CAPTURED IN WONDERLAND

WONDERLAND CHRONICLES
BOOK TWO

FoxTales Press

DANI HOOTS

Captured in Wonderland
Wonderland Series, #2
© 2020 FoxTales Press
Content edits by: Nightingale Proofreading
Proofreading by: Victory Editing
Cover Design Copyright © 2020 by Biserka
Designs
All rights reserved.

ISBN for paperback: 978-1-942023-77-7

ISBN for hardcover: 978-1-942023-78-4

"One of the deep secrets of life is that all that is really worth the doing is what we do for others."

— Lewis Carroll

Chapter 1

The bell rang, and everyone who wasn't already in their seats rushed to sit down before Mr. Barnes could scold them. He hated it when students weren't prepared for class the moment the clock struck 8 a.m.. I didn't quite understand this frustration as it was still early in the morning and not everyone was awake yet. I mean, I sure wasn't.

It bummed me out that we had Mr. Barnes again for English during our sophomore year, but at least all my friends made it into many of the same classes as me. I glanced over at Kate, who had her copy of *1984* open with diligent notes scribbled along the margins. Glancing at my book that had scattered notes, most not even having to do with the book but art ideas I had, I wished I was as put together as she was. However, I had a lot more on my plate than met the eye.

I had spent most of my time in Wonderland, searching for Morpheus and dealing with whatever minor evil we came across.

Actually, we mainly goofed off in Wonderland and had adventures in the different districts, so I couldn't act like I was really fighting crime or anything on the side, like in *Sailor Moon*. However, now I knew how they felt juggling school and the fantasy world. It was not easy. I was managing though, for the most part. Malcolm helped me with my homework and with studying. My cheeks felt a little warm thinking about him.

Glancing over at the two troublemakers in class, I found the backs of their shaggy brown hair. Although Davis's hair stayed the same color when we went to Wonderland, Chase's changed into a deep purple. I presumed he didn't keep it that color, as he would stand out more than he already did. No matter where he went in this world, he always seemed to cause trouble.

I wondered how Chase and Davis even managed not to annoy Mr. Barnes to the point where he forbade them to be in his class this year. But alas, it was spring now and Mr. Barnes hadn't had a complete breakdown. Yet. To be fair, it was mainly Chase causing problems and doing things he shouldn't be doing in this realm, such as hiding Mr. Barnes's coffee and making it reappear in random spots throughout the room by using his magic. Once, he'd hidden the cup on top of the projector, and Mr. Barnes about had a meltdown right then and there. It was entertaining, but I didn't enjoy having the entire class scolded because of something Chase had done.

Chase whispered something to Davis, who tried to ignore him, and I kicked Chase's chair.

Turning around to face me, he raised his eyebrow. "What?"

"Be quiet. Mr. Barnes is about to start class. You are going to get another detention and get kicked out."

He rolled his light brown eyes, which was a lot less dramatic than when they were golden catlike eyes. "It doesn't matter. I don't actually live here."

Chase had a point; none of the guys from Wonderland really needed to be in this realm or go to high school. I'd asked why they stayed around after we defeated Morpheus, but they never answered me and always dodged the question. I figured it had to do with the fact that Morpheus was still alive and they wanted to make sure he didn't attack me again. However, it has been over a year, and we have heard nothing from him in this realm or Wonderland.

"Well, either way, I want to graduate, and you like dragging me down with you sometimes. If I get another detention, my parents will probably kick me out."

He laughed. "You have only had one this year."

It was my turn to roll my eyes. "I know that, but you realize not many students actually get detention, right? Usually you just get lectured or talk to the advisor to see why you are acting out and all that."

"Fine, whatever. But in that instance, I wasn't at fault. How was I supposed to know we weren't allowed in there?"

"I think it was the sign that said Keep Out."

"Well, you went with me."

I stuck my tongue out. That was fair, but I didn't want to leave him and have something happen. Then he wouldn't have had anyone there to go get help. It was probably a stupid notion as he was the Cheshire cat.

Which was why he always got into trouble, whether it be in this world or another.

"Chase, you can talk to your friends on your own time. And since you seem to like to make noise, you can begin reading part three of *1984* on page 225 for us to examine," Mr. Barnes scolded, his exhausted blue eyes glaring at Chase.

"Yes, sir." Chase turned around and started reading from his book. "He did not know where he was…"

First period went by as slow as ever, and I couldn't wait to get to biology class. I didn't care for the class in particular, but that was where I got to meet up with

Malcolm. As I got out of English and hurried to my locker in the sophomore hall, I found him already next to it, waiting for me. His black hair was pulled back in a short ponytail, with long strands loose and outlining his face. I always wondered why he pulled it back when he still had hair in his face but never asked since it was handsome as heck. He leaned in and gave me a small kiss after checking to make sure no teachers were in the hallway.

Oh yeah, did I mention we were dating?

It happened over summer break when I spent way too much time in Wonderland versus the real world. He trained me in different fighting styles, of which I have been getting pretty good at. Then one day when we were practicing, I tripped and fell on him—anime style. Then we kind of kissed, and then the kiss turned into a make-out session that Davis walked in on. So since then, we have been together.

And it has been great.

"Ready for bio?" Malcolm asked as I switched out my books.

I nodded. "As ready as I can be. Don't we have to dissect sheep brains today?"

"That's what's on the syllabus."

Suddenly an arm appeared around Malcolm's shoulder and Chase smiled. "I will bet you all that Davis throws up in class."

"That's not fair!" Davis squeaked. "You know how I

get when we have to dissect something."

Chase looked at Malcolm. "Can I switch partners with you today?"

Both Malcolm and I answered in unison. "No."

Chase laughed as we headed toward biology. Kate took chemistry instead of biology, so we had a few different classes in our schedules. I was glad we had English and geometry together, however, as she helped me study for those classes. Studying with these guys never quite helped.

Malcolm and I took a seat at our lab table since we were, of course, lab partners. As long as we did our work, Mrs. Wisteria didn't seem to care who partnered. It surprised me she hadn't separated Chase and Davis, although Chase was a lot better behaved in this class. He learned early on not to get on Mrs. Wisteria's bad side.

Melvin was partnered with a girl by the name of Aya, who was clearly flirting with him, but he either didn't notice or just ignored her. Chase tried to bring it up once, but Melvin acted like he didn't know what he was talking about.

"All right, class." Mrs. Wisteria pulled back her curly, coffee-colored hair. "Today we are going to study the different parts of the brain. We will be slicing a sheep's brain to get a better look at how it is physically versus drawings and pictures that are modified to show things more clearly. Any questions?"

Chase raised his hand. "Can I have a different partner?"

Mrs. Wisteria ignored Chase's comment and went on with the lecture. I wished the manga and anime *Cells at Work!* went into more detail for the different organs as it would have been very helpful for this part of the term. But at least it got me through the cells and disease processes part of the quarter.

The TA started taking out the sheep brains from the buckets labeled Brains and laid them on our trays. I watched as Davis, who sat at the lab table in front of us, put his hand over his mouth. Yeah, he was going to barf. Chase totally called it. As the TA dumped the brain on their tray, Davis ran out of the classroom.

"Ugh!" Chase exclaimed. "This is why I wanted a different lab partner."

Mrs. Wisteria sighed. "He will be back after he throws up, Chase. Just start the lab without him."

I held back a laugh. I felt bad for Davis, but it was always fun to see Chase's reaction, and the fact that he had to do more work was always a bonus. He deserved it for the trouble he caused Davis in other classes.

As we began dissecting the brain, I had to agree with Davis—I wanted to barf too. I had to keep thinking about Malcolm and how I didn't want to seem weak in front of him. And the fact I doubted he would let me kiss him later if my breath smelled of vomit.

I had trained hard for the past year so I could be

strong and show that I didn't need protecting. I had come a long way, but I knew it was still nothing compared to what these guys could do. I had a lot of catching up to do if I was honest.

Would I ever catch up to them? They had centuries on me when it came to knowledge and fighting skill. I felt like an infant compared to them and tried not to think about the actual age difference. It definitely felt like an anime in that regard, as there were many animes where the main character was a lot older than they looked, like Jibril, the immortal angel from *No Game No Life*, or Holo, the wolf goddess from *Spice and Wolf*.

Second period came and went, and third period, US History, was a bore. I didn't care for US History but liked to learn more about the entire world. When we only went over the US, it made me think of all the flashbacks from *Hetalia* that were sad. So many episodes made me cry.

But the best part of the day was finally here: lunch. It was my favorite as I could actually talk to my friends without getting into trouble, and it was the only time Kate and I could hang out since she started taking track and field. She was fantastic at the long jump and three-thousand-meter long run. I watched a couple of her meets, and it was amazing to see her succeed and beat the other teams.

I took a seat at the table with Malcolm and handed

him the bento I'd made. I never imagined I would actually get to make a boy bento lunches. It was a dream come true, to say the least. He kissed my cheek and opened it.

"Flower-themed today. I love it," he said with a smile.

"I figured since the cherry trees are blooming, I would make some flower-themed ones."

"Well, it's beautiful. Thank you very much."

Kate took a seat across from me. "I don't know how you find the time to make yourself lunch like that."

I shrugged. "I get up early or stay up late to make them. I sleep like an artist, so it's fine."

Chase took a seat next to Kate. "I don't think it's fair. You don't make anything for the rest of us."

I raised an eyebrow. "That's because all you eat is tuna, and I don't like to cook tuna."

"I'd eat other stuff if it was made for me."

"Well, how about I make you all something next Monday? I'll come up with a recipe this weekend and bring one giant casserole dish. Does that sound good?"

Chase smiled. "It does."

Melvin and Davis took a seat next to Malcolm.

Melvin asked, "Did we miss anything?"

Chase nodded toward me. "She's going to make us a giant casserole dish of something yummy on Monday."

Melvin smirked. "Oh? So you are going to finally make the rest of us something to eat?"

Malcolm sighed. "That's enough. Stop making Alice feel bad. I will share my bento if all of you really feel left out."

Chase reached for the onigiri in Malcolm's bento and Malcolm hit Chase's hand with the chopstick. "Except you. You started this mess."

"Hey, that's not fair!"

The two of them started bickering, and I turned to Kate. "So, are we still up to go shopping downtown this weekend?"

She nodded. "Yeah, that would be great. We haven't gotten to hang out lately between my track and your dance." She glanced over at Malcolm and the others. "And your other distractions."

"Sorry about that. They can be a handful."

"I totally get it. I still can't believe you were able to beat all the other girls to get him. You were so sure you weren't even in his league."

I blushed. I did say that last year, but that was before I went to Wonderland and found out the truth. I was definitely a different person now due to that experience. There was so much to explore in both worlds, and I wanted to see it all. I took a bite of my omurice. Life was an adventure right now, and I wouldn't have it any other way.

Chapter 2

Becca clapped her hands. "Okay, class, start with your daily warm-ups. Everyone at the barre."

I went over with the other students to the barre and did our fifteen-minute warm-up, which consisted of grand pliés, single-leg relevés, and a lot of stretching on the floor. I found that stretching, besides helping with dance, helped in combat and swordsmanship. I was a lot more flexible than Melvin, for example, and could defeat him if we were in certain terrain that needed a little more flexibility rather than strength. He always acted like he let me win those times, but I called bull.

Chase took the spot next to me. I was able to convince him to take dance with me, and he seemed to enjoy it. He didn't make trouble here like he did at school, and I figured it was because he didn't want me to feel embarrassed for bringing someone who caused problems. It was my sanctuary, and I didn't want anyone to ruin it.

That, and Becca could be scary when she was pissed.

He was able to test through the different levels and join my level in no time. He was actually one of the best boy performers we had, which was saying a lot. He had a knack for keeping balance, and since he was already strong, he had no problem with carrying girls or landing silently. It amazed Becca he never took ballet before. We couldn't explain to her it was because he was a lot older than he appeared and because he was a cat. I don't think she would have even believed us.

We did our stretch routine and moved on to strengthen some of our ballet moves, mainly the sauter and pirouette. It may seem easy to spin in place, but it wasn't that simple. Not only do you have to master pointe but also be able to spin around in multiple rotations and not swing around or bob about. We practiced every lesson, but I still could barely manage one rotation without wobbling.

Becca watched us and gave us each some pointers. "Alice, you need to lift with your chest. Don't think about your legs as much as your chest bringing your body up and keeping it level."

I nodded as if I knew what she was talking about. I

honestly didn't. Chase tapped me on the arm.

"Like this, Alice." Chase did a pirouette with three rotations.

Becca clapped. "That was amazing, Chase! Now do three more sets."

He sighed and did as she asked as I tried to practice my one rotation. I stuck my tongue out at him when Becca's back was turned. He mimicked me, and we went on with our lesson.

Since I always had an hour to kill before my parents got off work, Chase and I went and bought something to drink at Broadway Coffee House. I usually ordered an herbal tea, but Chase always got a nitro, and I had to deal with hyper Chase. I didn't know how he slept at night or if he even did. I always thought cats needed more sleep than humans, but I guess that didn't matter when they were from Wonderland.

Taking a seat, I admired how hipster-like this place was. Most of the male workers had well-trimmed beards and man buns, and those who had glasses had thick-rimmed frames. The walls were painted gray and showcased art for sale. It was my dream to get some of my art on display like this, but I knew I was far from it.

It seemed like parts of Portland were slowly making its way down to Salem, and it was nice for those who hated this city. There was literally nothing to do here, and if one wanted to do anything fun, one needed a car, which I did not have yet. Soon though, since I had my permit and my parents were teaching me to drive. A few more months and I could drive myself. I couldn't wait.

Then Malcolm and I could go on dates whenever we wanted. In this world anyway. We got to do whatever we wanted in Wonderland.

"Are you still having trouble figuring out how to do the pirouette like Becca was talking about?" Chase asked as he sipped his drink.

I nodded. "Yeah, I just don't understand what she means by using my chest to lift myself up. I mean, isn't it my legs that are lifting me up?"

He shook his head. "No, you need to think of it more like a chain reaction. Here, let's go in the parking lot and I will show you."

We took our drinks outside and set them on the curb while we found a deserted part of the parking lot, as most of this was for the church during the weekend. Chase turned to me and placed his hand on his chest.

"Put your hand like this."

I nodded and did as he asked. "Okay, now what?"

"Now pretend you are lifting your chest with your hand. See how it moves your entire body up?"

"Kind of?"

He paused. "Let me think. You know how in *Yuri on Ice* where they always seem to be puffing out their chest while they skate?"

I smiled at his reference. I made him binge it a while back. "Yes?"

"Try to put yourself in their shoes. Ice skating is pretty much ballet on ice, and they have to lead with their chest as well. Think about it like that. Kind of like a string is attached and you are pulling yourself along."

I tried to imagine myself as Yuri, or Yurio, and spun around on my Converse. Although it wasn't the same as pointe shoes, I felt like I could connect with my body. I jumped up and down. "I did it!"

Chase held up his hand. "High five!"

I high-fived him and we laughed. "Thanks, Chase, you were a big help."

"Well, then maybe you will make me a bento tomorrow to say thanks." He grinned.

"Sure, I'll do that. Speaking of which, I better ride over to my parents' work. It's almost time to meet with them."

"Stay safe," he said as he watched me unlock my bike. Chase just transported wherever he needed and hoped no one would notice. He offered to transport me places, but I was hesitant. Mainly I didn't want someone to spot us but also because it made me a little sick to my stomach. However, when I was really late, I might have called upon his talents once or twice. Or when I forgot my slippers in my locker.

I rode over to my parents and only had to wait a few

minutes for them to pack up. I hooked my bike on the back of their silver Escalade, and we picked up some Michelangelo's for dinner. It was an Italian restaurant that had the best lasagna I have ever had. I haven't really left Salem much though, so for all I knew it could be terrible and I just didn't know. I couldn't wait until I graduated so I could get out of this place and explore the world… and try a variety of restaurants.

Even though it was rare for my parents to make dinner, since they both just got done with the busy season and were still too tired to cook for us, we all ate at the table. I didn't blame them. Sometimes they went to work so early that I was still up painting. I tried to hide the fact I was doing my hobby and acted like I was doing homework, but it was a lie.

Sitting down, I dug into my lasagna.

"How were both your days at school?" my mother asked.

I shrugged. "Same as normal."

"Staying away from that one kid who got you into detention?" my father asked.

No. "Yes."

"Good. I don't want you to do stupid things for some boy. You better not date someone like that."

Yeah, my parents didn't know about Malcolm, and there were a few reasons for that. The first one was because I didn't need them giving me crap about that being why my grades were slipping, if they slipped. So far, other than the detention, I was doing well. Thank you, Kate and Malcolm. Second was because I knew they would want to meet his parents, and well... he didn't really have any. How could I explain to them that my boyfriend lived in another world and didn't have any adult supervision? Yeah, that wasn't going to happen.

"What about you, Lilith?" mother asked my sister.

"Well, with racquetball season over, I've been studying after school with my classmates in Eugene's classroom. We took a practice test today and will go over the answers later this week."

I really didn't want to take AP classes. Life was tough already between juggling school, dance, having a boyfriend behind my parent's back, and fighting evil in Wonderland. It wasn't like I could explain that to them either and had a feeling next year they would make me sign up for AP classes like my sister. I couldn't wait.

Dinner went by calmly, which I was always thankful for. I didn't like it when I got into arguments with my sister, and luckily, since she was busy studying for tests, she left me alone. I kept to myself and painted, after I finished my homework of course.

Who am I kidding?

Since I was learning how to sketch figures, I decided to practice drawing ballet poses, which was very hard to do since they all looked like they weren't bending naturally. Before I knew it, it was two in the morning.

Crap, I needed to make bentos for tomorrow.

I had to choose. Make bentos now and not wake my parents, or go to sleep now and hopefully wake up early enough to make them? The decision was always a hard one to make.

Especially since I hadn't even done my US History homework yet.

Deciding I should do homework and then wake up early to make the bentos, I tried to work as fast as I could. I hoped at least half of it made sense as I crawled into my bed and passed out.

I was standing in the middle of a circus tent. Everything seemed silent; the bleachers were empty, and the storage cleared. All that was left was this dusty tent and soft blue light that seemed to be coming from the moon outside. Was this once the Nightmare Circus? Was I standing where fear once had taken over Wonderland?

I rubbed my eyes. No, I had been asleep in my room. I hadn't traveled back to Wonderland tonight. Was this a dream?

I tried to will myself to awaken from this dream, but it didn't work. I wished I had bought that lucid dreaming book I saw at the metaphysics store Kate and I dared each other to walk into. I felt it would have helped right about now. Deciding to abandon trying to wake up, I peered around for anyone. It didn't seem like anyone was in the tent, so I decided to check outside.

My shoes crunched on the gravel, and the smell of salty sea air filled my lungs. If I remembered correctly, there was no ocean near where the circus had resided. But I did remember an ocean when Morpheus took over my mind.

That place didn't exist in Wonderland. It had all been in my head and put there by Morpheus. Memories of the last time I was here came flooding into my mind. This couldn't be real—I couldn't be back here. I had defeated him. He had no control over me anymore.

"Oh, Alice, do you really think you are stronger than me?"

I slowly turned to find Morpheus standing behind me. He was different from when I had seen him a year ago. His once well-trimmed hair and face were now shaggy and ruffled. His blue ringleader coat was tattered and stained. I wouldn't have recognized him if it weren't for where I was.

"Morpheus…," I whispered.

He bowed. "One and the same. Pardon my look, but my life hasn't been the easiest after you destroyed my circus."

"You were destroying dreams. I don't feel sorry for you."

"And I don't want your pity. No, I want something far more valuable than that." He took a step closer and I stepped back.

"Oh, and what's that?" I asked as he took another step and I stepped closer to the cliff.

"I need you, Alice. I need you to help me restore Wonderland."

I let out a laugh. "As if I would help you. You tried to destroy Wonderland."

He shook his head while still advancing slowly. I turned to find I had nowhere else to go. I was trapped between him and the cliffside.

"Dear Alice, you are capable of so many things in Wonderland, you have no idea. Your dear Hatter doesn't want to tell you the truth."

I blushed. How did he know we were a couple? "What do you mean?"

He was only inches away from me now. "You have the power to mold Wonderland into whatever you want it to be, just like the original Alice. It is a power only chosen humans can do. You have so much power, yet it is being wasted away while you are in the mortal realm, doing nothing but going to school and dance."

The fact he knew what I did in the mortal realm frightened me. "How do you know so much about what goes on outside Wonderland?"

He laughed. "Silly Alice, you underestimate my power. Now, it is time for you to wake up."

With that, he shoved me off the cliff and into the roaring ocean below.

Chapter 3

I woke up to find my Tardis alarm clock wheezing as it did every morning. I checked the time. It was six.

Dragging my legs to the side of the bed, I started shaking. What the heck was that nightmare? Why did I dream of Morpheus after all this time? I hadn't had a dream about him since I first was in Wonderland. Was it just a coincidence?

But it felt so real.

When I came back to the real world the first time, I had thought it was a dream as well, as barely any time passed in this world. This felt the same—as if I had transferred to another world and came back. My body hurt, I was shaking, and fear touched every nerve.

Glancing around my room, I found it exactly how I left it. Nothing seemed off about it, so I wondered if everything that had happened was just in my head. How would I have traveled to Wonderland without Chase or the mirror the White Rabbit uses? It made little sense.

Taking in a deep breath, I let it out slowly. It was just a dream—there was no reason to be afraid. I needed to focus on the now and not think about him, even though I knew he was still on the loose. We would find him eventually. All of Wonderland wanted revenge for what he did.

It impressed me he could stay hidden for so long. Most people in Wonderland believed he was in the Dark Forest, but Malcolm and Melvin had swept the entire area. There was no trace of him.

Shaking my head, I decided it was better to move on with my life and forget about the dream. I needed to make three bentos this morning, and time was wasting. I also needed to do some homework during lunch as I remembered I forgot to do geometry problems. At least I knew Kate could help me with those.

I debated on what theme to make the bentos today while I quickly took a shower and changed into an anime shirt and jeans. Chase seemed interested in the onigiri I had made the day before, so I decided to do another sakura-themed bento. Opening the pantry, I grabbed the bag of rice and went to work, careful to measure out how much water and rice I needed. It was important to get the ratio so that there wasn't extra water, or not enough. Unlike that BBC cooking show, I did not strain my rice after it cooked.

That video was cringeworthy.

Shaking my head at the thought of it, I put the pot on the stove and started on the other parts of the meal while the rice cooked.

"Wow, Alice, I didn't think you would actually make me one!" Chase opened the bento and smiled. "Thanks a lot!"

I handed the other bento to Malcolm.

"Don't you know better than to spoil a cat? Then he will never leave you alone," Malcolm said as he opened his box.

"Hey! That's not nice!" Chase yelled.

"He helped me with some dance moves yesterday, so it's a thank-you meal," I explained. "So he deserves it today."

Chase stuck his tongue out at both of us. Kate took a seat next to him. She looked out of place with us, as she dressed rather nicely with a designer shirt and skirt, whereas the guys and I dressed in graphic tees, a hoodie, and jeans. Since I painted a lot and got it all over myself more times than not, I tended not to want to spend too much money on clothes. It made me sad when I got ink or paint on my Sesshomaru shirt. Now it will be stained forever.

"What did I miss?" she asked as she blew on her

leftover casserole. Mrs. B loved making casseroles since they had a good mix of meat and vegetables and because she was superb at making them. The weekends were always great when I got to eat at their house. I wished my parents cooked at home more often.

Chase held up his bento. "I'm special today! I got a bento!"

"Wow, it's the sign of the apocalypse. We are probably all going to die now."

Chase frowned. "Why is everyone so mean to me?"

Davis took a seat on the other side of Chase. "Because you are mean to all of us. I say it serves you right after what you said in English today."

Chase snickered. "You had it coming. You started tearing up because the character was being tortured."

"It wasn't fair! He did nothing wrong! He wanted to help the world, only to be betrayed and beaten."

"I take it we are finishing *1984* today?" Malcolm asked. It was a bummer we weren't in the same class, but I suppose some distance made the heart fonder. Yes, I was a sappy teenager. Get over it.

I nodded. "Yup. It's a sad ending, but I'm not sure it was crying worthy."

He slapped his hand on the table. "I wasn't crying!"

Melvin took a seat next to me. "You ran out of biology yesterday throwing up. I don't have to be in English to know you were definitely crying."

Davis put his head on the table. "You all are so mean."

I poked his arm. "Would an onigiri make you feel better?"

His head shot up. "Does it have cheese?"

I sighed. "No, but it has a pickled plum."

"I guess that's still okay."

He took one of my onigiri and munched on it. Chase looked at Malcolm. "Oh, so no comment about him getting spoiled?"

Malcolm shrugged. "He deserves it more than you."

Chase rolled his eyes and went back to eating his bento. He didn't make a peep about any of the food items, so I guess it was true he didn't mind eating things other than fish. It made me smile a little, then I remembered the important thing I needed to do at lunch.

I turned to Kate. "Hey, can you help me with geometry homework? I may or may not have forgotten to do it last night. I got some done during bio today but not all of it. Some were kind of hard."

Kate nodded. "Yeah, I can help. Let me see what you have so far."

I pulled the homework out of my *Sailor Moon* backpack and gave it to her. She scoured the paper.

"I see what your problem is." She pointed at some of my scribbles. "Right here you forgot to take in account that it isn't a square but a trapezoid. Just use this equation." She wrote the equation out. "And you should be set."

That made sense. She always made it seem easy, but at least she could put it into terms I understood.

"Thank you so much, Kate! I should be able to finish the other question quickly now."

"No problem. Just remember to finish your homework before you paint. You wouldn't be crunching on time as much."

She knew me too well. "I'll try. It's just less fun that way."

"Yeah. Sure. But I need to get going, I have a meeting with my track teammates. See you in math later."

"Yeah. See ya!"

She left the table, and I was left with the troublemakers. I looked at them all and sighed.

"Hey, what was that sigh for?" Chase asked.

"Nothing. Just that I know you are going to start something later today in a class. You always do."

"Thank you."

Malcolm shook his head. "That was not a compliment."

They started arguing, and their conversation blurred in my mind as I saw someone at the entrance to the cafeteria. He had shaggy hair, a tattered coat, and a dusty top hat.

Morpheus.

I felt like I couldn't breathe. What the heck was

going on? I blinked and suddenly he was gone, but my head felt as if it were spinning. I tried to gasp for air, but nothing was coming.

"Alice, are you all right?" Malcolm asked.

I shook my head as I kept trying to gasp for air. Finally it came and I coughed. Glancing back up, I found him to be gone.

"What happened? Was something stuck in your throat?" Chase asked.

"No... I don't... I saw..." I didn't know how to explain what I saw. "Morpheus. I think he somehow traveled to the mortal realm."

Malcolm shook his head. "That's impossible. We would have known."

I shrugged. "He was in my dream last night, and it seemed very real. Then I swore I just saw him standing in the doorway."

Chase shrugged. "It could have been your imagination."

"But I felt him. I couldn't breathe and..." I knew I should have told them earlier, but I had been too afraid of how they would react. "Last night I dreamed I was in Wonderland and he had me trapped in my mind again. When I woke, I was shaking and I just figured it was a nightmare. But in my dream he seemed so real. Maybe he is back."

Malcolm responded, "He can't come to this world without the White Rabbit or Chase, and we know it wasn't either of them. It was probably just a dream. It makes little sense he would try anything now."

"Yeah... I guess you're right."

Chase frowned. "It's possible, since he thinks he's the god of dreams, that he could enter through her dreams. Perhaps he was using all that time to get enough power and attack Alice that way."

We were all silent. Could Morpheus actually travel straight into my dreams, and it took him this long to gather up enough strength?

Melvin pitched in. "Maybe we should go to Wonderland and check in with the others. The king and queen might know what to do."

"Yeah, maybe we should do that. They might know something," I said.

Malcolm wrapped his arm around me. "Don't worry. He can't get to you. I will make sure of that."

I smiled and leaned against his shoulder. I was thankful he was my guardian, but that wouldn't stop Morpheus from being able to enter my dreams. I didn't know what to do.

Especially when Morpheus said Malcolm was hiding information from me—information about my role in Wonderland.

I was a few minutes early, and I took a seat and pulled out my homework. I still had problems to solve and seven minutes to solve them. With Kate's equation, I knew I could manage it as long as Chase didn't distract me with some kind of prank. Glancing over, I found him doodling in his notebook.

The sad part was that if I tried to do the homework last night, it would have taken much longer. It's funny how much faster one could work when it was crunch time.

I finished my homework right when the bell sounded. I hurried back to my seat after handing in the papers I hoped were legible enough for Mr. Yamata to read. Sometimes he commented on my handwriting not being that great, which everyone found ironic since I was an artist. Just because I could draw did not mean I took enough time to work on my penmanship.

Taking a seat next to Kate, I opened up my textbook. "How did your meeting go?"

She shrugged. "Good. They think we will go to State this year."

"That would be so cool! I'm glad you have a sport you are great at. I have dance, but other than that, I don't really have anything going for me."

She bit her lip. "I wonder if it's because you hang out around those guys too much."

Her comment took me by surprise. I didn't think she minded Malcolm and the others, so it came out of nowhere. "I mean, we hang out, but I don't know if it would be too much."

"I just think… Never mind, forget I said anything."

Before I could respond, Mr. Yamata started the class.

I decided to let it go and maybe see if she would go into detail this weekend when we would have our sleepover.

That is, if I was brave enough to.

Chapter 4

We all met after school near Chase's locker. No one seemed to hang around, as technically no students were allowed to wander around the campus without a pass, and because no student in their right mind would want to stay around this place of dread longer than they had to. As we gathered, I glanced at Chase's locker. It appeared normal enough, like all the other gray lockers in the hallways, but I knew the truth—it's what they used to travel to Wonderland.

One may ask why we had to go through the locker instead of any doorway to get to Wonderland, and that was a good question. Apparently this gate was always open and was easier on Chase since it took a lot of energy to create portals between different worlds. But since it was in his locker, I always wondered where

Chase kept his books.

"Ugh, I hate this part," I commented as Chase opened his locker. In front of us was the gel-like, shimmery goo that reminded me of *Stargate SG-1*.

Chase wrapped his arms around me in a quick motion and fell back into the locker, laughing. "Down we go!"

I shrieked, even though I knew it was coming. He always liked to grab me and toss me in like that. I think it was mainly because I screamed every single time.

Falling down and down and down was always the worst. I didn't understand why it took so long and why we had to endure this feeling, but I guess it was like having to take a car ride from home to school. There was no way to travel a distance without some time passing by. However, traveling to a different world like this disobeyed what I felt were the laws of physics, so maybe I was wrong. It wasn't like science was my best subject.

We hit the soft, grassy ground, and I found myself in the weird room we always transported to. I queried everyone on why it was this place in the Garden District that it always dumped us out into, but no one had a clear answer. Chase could take us home through any doorway he wanted, and he didn't always appear in front of his locker, but for some reason when he took any doorway from Earth to Wonderland, we always appeared in this spot. It made no sense.

Then again, nothing about Wonderland made sense. A few moments later, Malcolm, Melvin, and Davis appeared.

Malcolm glared at Chase. "Stop making my girlfriend scream like that."

Chase shrugged. "I'm just having fun. Besides, it's something we do in dance class all the time, isn't it, Alice?"

I sighed as I noticed Malcolm frown at the fact that Chase spends more time with me after school. "Yeah, you guys like picking me up when I least expect it to hear me squeal."

He laughed. "You make the cutest noise!"

I blushed and turned away from both Malcolm and Chase. "Shouldn't we get going to see the king and queen? What time is it here anyway?"

Pushing the door open, I found that it was nighttime.

Malcolm stepped up next to me and wrapped his arm around my waist. "It seems to be just past midnight. We will have to wait for the morning before we can talk to the king and queen."

"How much time will have passed in the real world if we wait until tomorrow?"

He shrugged. "Probably only five minutes, ten minutes tops."

"That's good. I should still have half an hour to spare before my sister's study session is over. She is supposed to drive me home, and if I'm not next to her car in time, she'll leave me."

"You have an interesting family, Alice."

"Interesting doesn't even begin to cover it." I debated what would happen if my parents found out how I spent my spare time. Would I be grounded? "Well, where should we stay for the night?"

Chase shoved past me and into the street. "Wherever we want! This is Wonderland!"

Melvin and Davis walked out of the weird shed room as well.

Melvin began, "Chase, just transport us to the palace please. I want my own bed."

"Ugh, fine. But before you get any ideas, Hatter, Alice is sleeping in her own room."

I felt my face turn red. I couldn't believe he would say that. I mean, we were once caught up late in his room, but we were just talking. I didn't realize how late it had gotten.

"I'm a gentleman. A street cat like you wouldn't understand what that means."

"Yeah, whatever. Do you all want to be transported or not?"

We all hung on to each other, and Chase transported us in the middle of the Dream Palace's corridors. The beauty of this place always amazed me. I gaped at the intricate satin murals that depicted Wonderland's history. There was even a new one that showed my fight against Morpheus. I was so embarrassed about it and hated it when people in the kingdom talked about it. I didn't feel like I was a hero, no matter how many times they told me I was.

Within moments of us arriving, fifteen guards pointed their swords at us.

"Chill! It's us!" Chase exclaimed as he yawned. "And we are tired."

"You know better than to appear in the middle of the palace, Chase. You are supposed to sign in at the front gate so we know you are here." Bill stepped out in front of his men. "If the White Rabbit wasn't preoccupied, he would have shot you without a second thought."

Bill was tall with a smirk that never left his lips. He had a handsome face, and I was glad it wasn't shrouded in darkness any longer. A couple of seconds later, Kenny stumbled over next to him.

"It's late. Why are you so loud?" Kenny asked as he rubbed his eyes.

Bill turned to him. "If you're tired, then go to sleep."

Kenny wrapped his arms around him. "But I can't sleep without you by my side."

Bill rolled his eyes and turned to us. "It's nice to see you again, Malcolm. Do you have anything to report?"

Malcolm nodded. "In a way, but I'll wait to explain it all in the morning. I want to talk to the king and queen as well."

"Understood. You know where your quarters are."

Kenny glanced at Malcolm. "Can I sleep with you then?"

"No."

Kenny pouted and went off with Bill. Malcolm turned to me. "I hope you don't mind waiting."

I shook my head. "No, I don't. I need to catch up on some sleep anyway since I didn't get much last night."

"Morpheus shouldn't be able to enter your dreams here, so you will be safe to rest as long as you need. If you need anything, just come get me."

I nodded. "Of course."

We each went to our own rooms. My room in the palace differed greatly from the one on Earth. I kept the necessities I would need here, such as clothing, swords, and a stuffed Eevee from Build-A-Bear that I could snuggle with. I slept with a Pikachu at home and wanted something else to hold while I was here. It connected me to the real world, and because after sleeping with a stuffed animal for so long, my arms didn't know what to do without one, and I couldn't sleep.

Changing into some pajamas, I realized that this was actually a real world, and I needed to stop referring to my realm as real. A lot of people here didn't like it when I said that. I guess I would be a little irritated if someone kept referring to my home as not real as well.

I lay down on my soft satin sheets and stared at the wooden ceiling. Soon we would figure out what was going on with me and find where Morpheus was hiding. All would be wondrous in Wonderland, pun intended.

Snuggling my Eevee, I turned to my side and let my brain stop running a marathon. A few deep breaths and I was fast asleep.

"Alice...," a masculine voice beckoned. "Alice."

I opened my eyes to find myself in the middle of the Dark Forest. It was dark with light only from some of the plants and trisings, the strange little light fairy things, in the distance. The air clung to my skin—muggy but cool. I could barely breathe and I felt my heart begin to race. My eyes darted around, but I saw no one.

"Come here, Alice."

My bare feet stepped across the moss that covered the ground. At least I hoped it was moss as there was so much lingering fog near the ground I couldn't see my feet. I had no idea how I found myself in such a place as just moments ago I swore I was in the palace. Maybe I had been wrong—maybe this was where I had been the entire time.

Everything felt fuzzy as I kept forward, trying to figure out where the voice was coming from. I still couldn't see anything, and tears escaped my eyes. Why was this happening? How could I be here all alone with some voice calling me?

"Come to me, Alice."

I continued forward, not quite sure where in the Dark Forest I was at. I had only come here the one time to escape Bill and his men and defeat Morpheus. I recognized nothing other than it was all creepy and I knew I was somewhere in the Dark Forest.

"Alice…"

A figure formed in front of me, and I found that it was Morpheus. Then I realized what had happened—he had entered my dreams once again. "You!"

He laughed. "Of course it is me, Alice. Who else can enter your mind so easily?"

I frowned. I didn't like that I kept finding myself at his mercy. "It won't work this time. I know this is just a dream."

"Is it now? You are in Wonderland, and there have been many times where you have been transported all over the land. How do you know I didn't just do the same thing?"

"Because Chase is the only one who can transport people."

"Are you sure? There is a lot you still don't know about Wonderland. It is possible that someone else could transport you across the land, is it not?"

He had me there. Even after all my time in Wonderland, there were still a lot of secrets I hadn't found the answers to. If Chase could transport people and Bill had that apparatus that made it so he could reopen portals, what's to say that there isn't someone else who could do it?

But the question still remained: Was this all in my head or was this real? Was there a difference in the end?

Morpheus pulled out his sword from his cane. "And now, Alice, I must do what is right for Wonderland. I must kill you."

My eyes widened. "What?"

"You destroyed my dream, Alice. And like every other dream in Wonderland, there must be vengeance for those who destroy them."

I shook my head. "That makes little sense. I had to stop you because you were killing other dreams in Wonderland! You had to be stopped or Wonderland would have been destroyed!"

He shrugged. "I don't make the rules."

Morpheus lunged forward, and I quickly jumped back. I was still in my nightshirt and shorts and had nothing I could attack him with. I turned and started running deep into the forest. I didn't care where I was going, as long as it was away from the mad man with the sword.

Tree branches snagged my skin, and my feet found sharp rocks, causing blood to trickle down my arms and legs, but I didn't falter. I had to get out of here before it was too late—before Morpheus had his revenge.

As I kept on running, I found myself at the edge of a cliff. Crap, not again.

I turned to find Morpheus smiling. "Looks like it is the end of the line for you, Alice."

He moved closer toward me and I stumbled back. I lost my footing and started to fall when I felt something grab my arm.

"Alice! Snap out of it!" a voice called out. It was not Morpheus but someone familiar.

It was Malcolm's voice.

I blinked and suddenly I no longer was surrounded by fog but was now looking up at Malcolm, who held my arm. He was standing on the balcony of the palace. Glancing down, I found the thrashing ocean below.

I screamed.

"Grab my other hand!"

Scrambling, I did as he asked, and he was able to pull me back up onto the balcony. Malcolm wrapped his arms around me, and I clutched at his nightshirt. More tears fled from my eyes.

Malcolm stroked my head and kissed it. "It's okay, Alice. You are safe now."

I nodded but was still shaking from everything that happened. Morpheus made me sleepwalk and forced me to jump off this balcony with images of the Dark Forest.

I had almost jumped to my death—I had sleepwalked where I was running in my dream. How was that even possible?

It meant only one thing: Morpheus was still alive and he was playing with my head.

Chapter 5

"And that is what happened, Your Majesty." I told the queen and king everything that happened last night and the night before. I gave them detailed notes on what Morpheus looked like, where we were, what he said to me—all of it. I knew leaving out even the smallest detail could be detrimental.

The queen was wearing an intricate kimono with dragonfly patterns throughout. It had the entire spectrum of the color wheel, and I had to stop gaping. It was a masterpiece, and I wished I could talk to the seamstress to find out how she came across such fabric. Then I would have her teach me how to sew. The king had a matching one; however, his was black and white. It went well with their dynamic, I felt.

"If it weren't for the Duchess, who was out for her

early-morning stroll, I wouldn't have been there to save her," Malcolm explained.

Apparently the Duchess had run to his room to alert him of the trance I was under. I would have to thank her later.

"This is very troubling indeed." The queen turned to the king. "We are terrified to think about what Morpheus will try to do next."

"The first thing to do is have Bill go to the mortal realm and survey around. If Morpheus is somehow transporting there, he will be able to figure out where he is coming from," the king declared.

The thought of Bill traveling to my world was rather amusing. He reminded me of Jack Harkness from *Torchwood*, and I wondered how many people he would flirt with. He was going to cause trouble. I just knew it.

The queen nodded. "I agree. He will figure out if Morpheus is indeed traveling to your world or not. In the meantime, we will have our men survey Wonderland again to see if anyone has seen or heard anything in relation to Morpheus. Someone has to know something."

"I agree," the White Rabbit commented from his corner. It was strange that someone who looked like a little kid had such a high military ranking, but nothing really made sense in Wonderland. He had white blond hair and wore a light beige suit with a golden bow tie.

In all the times I had visited, I had never seen him leave the king and queen's side. I wondered if it was because it was his job, or if it had to do with feeling responsible for not keeping the king and queen safe during Morpheus' attack. "I can stay here and be on guard, so Bill will have nothing to worry about."

The queen turned to us. "Malcolm, I presume you and your unit want to stay with Alice?"

He nodded. "Yes. I feel I can keep her safe if I am close."

"No offense, Malcolm, but you haven't been able to keep her safe thus far and barely saved her only because of someone's help." The queen frowned. "I feel you are slipping, and I wonder why."

"I was getting too comfortable with the peace that we were experiencing, and I was caught off guard. It won't happen again."

"Be careful, Mad Hatter," the king added. "Love can also impede one's decision."

I felt a bit awkward as I didn't expect Malcolm to be reprimanded like that. I felt like it was my fault since we were a couple and growing closer. Was I the reason he wasn't paying enough attention to the task at hand?

The doors opened and the rest of the crew, along with Bill and Kenny, stepped in.

"Start the meeting without us, did you?" Melvin crossed his arms. "And here I thought we were all in this together."

Malcolm sighed. "There was an issue this morning, so we were awake far before you were."

Chase rushed over. "What happened? Did something happen to you, Alice?"

I nodded. "It was Morpheus. He was able to enter my dreams again. But everything is fine now."

Chase turned to Malcolm. "How is that possible?"

He shrugged. "I'm as frustrated about it as you are, if not more. She almost fell into the ocean."

Chase's eyes widened. "What? Why didn't you wake us?"

"Well, first off, because I had to act fast. Second, I took Alice somewhere so she could calm down. And now we are here."

Chase frowned but didn't add anything.

"Alice, I'm so glad you are all right." Davis wrapped his arms around me. "I don't know what I would have done if anything had happened to you."

Although he meant it in a good way, a thought struck me. This wasn't the first time they had lost Alice. These men were used to fighting in wars and losing those who had been close to them. They had lost Howard, their mentor. They were from Wonderland, which differed completely from Earth.

Which meant there was going to be a day when I left them.

It didn't mean I would die, but how long were they going to stick around on Earth? How long was I going to be able to return to Wonderland? It wasn't like the original Alice came here after she grew up, so did that mean I wouldn't be allowed to come here once I was an adult? Why did that suddenly hit me?

"Is something wrong?" Malcolm asked.

I shook my head. "No. I am just wondering why this is happening all of a sudden."

Bill interjected. "My theory is that Morpheus finally has enough energy again to wreak havoc. When the circus was happening, he had a lot of power he manifested from everyone's fear. Alice destroyed that source, so he had to wait to slowly gather more. I doubt he is close to being as influential as he once was, but as we can see, he is still a threat."

"Which brings me to your assignment, Bill." The queen opened her hand, and a scroll appeared out of nowhere. Magic was awesome here. "I want you to go to Earth and watch over Alice. Survey the land and make sure no extra portals are being opened."

He nodded. "Yes, Your Highness."

Kenny jumped up and down. "Oh, oh, oh! Can I go too?"

"Will you promise to stay out of trouble?" The queen asked.

"I promise!"

"Then I will allow it."

The White Rabbit whispered just enough so I could hear him, "that gets him out of my hair."

I also heard Malcolm moan as quietly as he could. I held back a chuckle. I didn't mind Kenny. I thought he was fun, but I didn't know what was going to happen when he was in the mortal realm.

Whatever it was, it was going to be a lot of fun.

We headed out of the throne room and into the corridor. A woman with a large gold-colored French dress stood as if waiting for us. Her hair was almost a golden blond and in tight curls. Her face was white with makeup, and her lips were a bright red. She reminded me of a French aristocrat.

"Malcolm, I am so glad you were able to save our dear Alice!" She grabbed me by the shoulders and kissed each cheek.

This must be the Duchess. Given her appearance, it made sense.

"And I am so thankful you alerted me to the situation," Malcolm commented.

She held me tight. "I would have been so upset if something happened to Alice. She is so beautiful and youthful. She is capable of so much."

"I, uh, thank you for saving me."

The Duchess shook her head. "No, no, thank you for saving Wonderland from the scary Morpheus. I don't know what I would have done if I had to stay in that fearful state. That black mask made everything I wore so dreary. It was the least I could do when you do so much for us."

Malcolm pulled me away from her, for which I was glad. It was strange being so close to someone I knew nothing about. "And I am glad you are safe as well, Duchess. But if you would please excuse us, we are heading back to the mortal realm before Alice is late."

"Oh yes, yes, of course! You take care of her, dear Hatter. She is the star of Wonderland."

As quickly as he could, he left the Duchess standing there.

"Do you not like her?" I asked.

He shrugged. "Something about her makes me uneasy. It could just be because of her loyalty to the past queens. She was always kissing up to whoever was ruling. I don't trust people like that."

That made sense to me. But she seemed sweet enough. I wished I could talk to her and learn more about the history of this place.

Then it hit me. We had a US History test tomorrow. Crap.

The first bell rang, and we got to our seats. Mr. Barnes wasn't in class yet, which was surprising. He was always here way before the bell rang. I once got to school an hour early due to my sister needing to study for some stupid test, and he was already in his class, waiting. He wasn't even grading but simply sitting at his desk, staring at the clock. It was strange.

Mr. Barnes finally walked in with another person in

tow. I wished I hadn't just drunk some water as I had spat it all on the back of Chase's head.

I could see the hair on Chase's neck lift as he spun around and just stared at me.

"I'm sorry…"

Davis held back his laughter but not enough as Mr. Barnes gave him an icy glare.

"That is enough laughing. I have an important announcement. I would like you to meet your new student teacher, Mr. Knave. Usually I don't have a student teacher, especially this time of the year, but the administration demanded it. He will be helping you go over what you learned from *1984*." Mr. Barnes nodded to Chase. "Watch out for this one. He is a troublemaker."

Kenny smiled. "Oh, I bet."

Chase raised his hand.

Kenny pointed at him. "You, troublemaking boy I have never met before, do you have a question?"

"May I go to the bathroom and dry off?"

Kenny turned to Mr. Barnes, who shook his head. Kenny slammed his hand on Chase's desk. "No. Now, other students, does anyone want to tell me what they have learned about *1984*?"

Pete, a blond, six-foot-tall, straight-A student, raised his hand. "I learned that no matter how hard you try, and no matter where your heart is at, sometimes the hero doesn't win and that the government sucks."

"Pfff. Nonsense." Kenny laughed. "The hero always wins and restores balance in the government."

Davis piped. "No, Mr. Knave, in the book the main character who was trying to do good is tortured for it."

Kenny frowned. "Tortured?"

Davis nodded. "Yup."

Kenny appeared as if he would cry. "That's horrible!"

"That's what I said!"

I glanced around the class, who all seemed perplexed that such a person could have the brain cells to teach our class. Kate appeared as confused as I was about this development. She, however, didn't know Kenny. This was going to be a really long rest of the quarter.

Malcolm was waiting for me at my locker. I hurried to him and gave him a hug.

"English was that bad, huh?"

I buried my head into his shoulder. "Oh my God, Malcolm. You won't believe it."

"Kenny is the new student teacher?"

I backed up and looked at him. "How did you know?"

He shrugged. "I was the one who got him the position."

I smacked him. "Why didn't you warn us?"

"I wanted to see your reaction."

"I spat water all over Chase."

He laughed. "Oh, now I wish I had seen that. Well, then I will warn you of the next surprise. Bill is our new PE teacher."

"He's our what?"

Sure enough, Bill was at PE. He made us call him Mr. L. I guess it stood for Lizard since, for some reason, in the original *Alice's Adventures in Wonderland*, he was a lizard. I couldn't imagine him being anything like how Lewis Carroll portrayed him. That guy got a lot of Wonderland wrong.

After our initial stretching, we went outside as it was warm enough to play kickball. I was excited since I was on the same team as Malcolm and Kate. Kate was fast, of course, and Malcolm was pretty strong and could kick the ball way into the outfield. I was... okay at it.

Bill, who was supposed to be just refereeing, decided he wanted in on the action as well. He took sides with Chase and Melvin, mostly because he wanted to go against Malcolm.

This would not end well.

Bill was pitching and Malcolm was the kicker. "Well, Malcolm, we will finally see who is the best."

"At kickball?"

"Kickball is life. I read the PE handbook."

Yeah, this conversation didn't seem weird at all. At least most of the students couldn't hear them bicker like this.

Malcolm asked straight-faced, "Is it a foul if I kick it at you?"

"I would like to see you try."

Bill rolled the ball, and Malcolm kicked it straight at Bill's stomach. Bill went down fast. We all rushed to him.

"Mr. L, are you okay?" I asked. After a few moments, he started laughing.

"I need to stop underestimating you, Malcolm. Also, by the way, go to the principal's office."

Malcolm sighed and headed toward the building. I felt a bit bad for him, but he had just kicked a ball straight into what was technically a teacher's stomach. I doubt he would get into too much trouble, as he would just tell them it was an accident.

Or at least I hoped.

Chapter 6

The weekend was here and so was hanging out with Kate. I was pretty excited as we hadn't been able to spend time together for a few weeks with just the two of us due to her track meets and some of the Wonderland-related things I needed to do. That, and sometimes Malcolm and I planned a weekend date. Those were always hard since my parents didn't know I had a boyfriend. I felt bad not letting them know, but I had good reason.

Today we decided to shop around downtown and then Mrs. B would pick us up, then her family and I were going mini golfing at the Best Little Roadhouse, have dinner there, and then pick up some cake at the Konditorei to eat at their place while we watch a movie. We still hadn't decided on what movie, but I guessed it would be a comedy.

We entered our usual place of interest, which was an antique shop by the name of Engelberg Antiks. My favorite part of the store was looking at all the old German steins, but I couldn't afford any even though some of them were rather cheap.

I glanced over at the occult section, happy they sold the haunted doll. That thing gave me nightmares. I swore it was always looking at me, and after hearing stories from the owner, I was too afraid to take a picture of it, as if the spirit could somehow follow me home. Anything was possible for spirits.

Kate flipped through the old records they kept. Sometimes they had some pretty cool 1980s records, and Kate collected them since her family had a record player. I thought it was really neat and asked my parents for one, but they said I had an iPhone so I didn't need one. I decided when I moved out I would just get one myself and play whatever I wanted whenever I wanted.

"Find anything good?" I asked.

She shook her head. "No, not today."

"Bummer."

"What else do you want to look at?" she asked as she tucked her hair behind her ear.

"Let's check out the clothes!"

We ventured to the back of the shop where most of the clothes were. One of these days I wanted to buy a dress and go to a masquerade, like something out of *The Great Gatsby*. I hadn't read the novel yet but saw the movie with Kate. I was looking forward to senior year though, when we went over it. The imagery was cool, and I wished I could go to dances and parties like they did. Maybe there would be something like that in Wonderland. One could always hope.

The dress I loved was still available. It was a red dress with loose strings all over it like something from the 1920s. I wanted it but always used my allowance on manga and paint supplies. One of these days I would remember to save up and buy it, or something similar.

"You just need to buy it."

I turned to Kate and laughed. "I know, right? Just remind me not to spend all my money at the art department." I held up my shopping bag from there, hearing the pens and brushes clack together, and smiled.

"I try, but you never seem to listen."

"Hey, it's not my fault Copics are so expensive. Even with the discount they have there."

"So you keep saying."

I laughed as we ventured downstairs to the basement. The basement had even more items but also a bunch of furniture. Near the back, however, I always got an eerie feeling and stayed away even if there was something cool to look at. It took me a while to shake off that energy.

I ran over to the mail-sorting furniture. "Wow, this is still here! I would totally buy it to hold my art supplies when I move out if it's still here! Maybe it will be on sale then!"

"How would a mail room desk be used to store art supplies?" Kate asked.

"Simple, I would just put different markers and paint and brushes in the different shelves. Easy as that."

She chuckled. "Only you would think of that."

"Hey, I'm practical."

She rolled her eyes as we looked at the various things throughout the basement. Near the back, I always felt a chill go down my spine, and I swear I heard someone walking up the steps that went to nowhere. I tried to move Kate along faster in that area because I didn't want to linger.

Once we had finished looking through the different items, we headed back outside. We turned to go to the café and grab something to drink like we normally did when we had sleepovers. I ordered an italian soda and Kate ordered a London Fog. A few moments later and our drinks were ready.

"What should we do next?" I asked as I took a chomp of the whipped cream on top. I swear that was the best part of an italian soda.

She shrugged. "I don't know, what do you want to

do?"

I pondered for a moment. "Well, we already know that I have all the anime shirts from Hot Topic."

"This is true."

I took a sip of my caramel-flavored soda. "Hey, do you think your mom could pick us up early? Then maybe we could go to Escape Fiction! I still have some credit and am willing to share if you can get your mom to take us. We will just have to finish our drinks before we go in."

Kate pulled out her Google phone. "You have yourself a deal."

Escape Fiction was the best place on Earth, hands down. They had so many books and in such a small space. I loved it. I could get lost in the maze of bookshelves. Once I did get lost and had to call for Kate to come rescue me. The owner made fun of me for it.

The owners, Scott and Maria, were an awesome couple who loved books, talking about books, and talking about anything really. I enjoyed sci-fi, which surprised him since few teenage girls came in to read classics like Isaac Asimov and Ray Bradbury. He had definitely given me a lot of recommendations over the years.

"What section first?" Kate asked.

"Uh, sci-fi and fantasy! Are there any other

sections?"

She laughed as we made our way through the books. There were just so many that I had no idea what I should get today. Going through all the books was such a task. I swore there were thousands upon thousands.

Except there was little to no manga. It had grown a little over the years, but it wasn't like Uwajimaya in Beaverton. Unfortunately there was nowhere to buy manga in Salem, and I had to either order it or save up a bunch of money and make a Uwajimaya and Barnes and Noble run up north with Kate and her mother. Then I would have to hide it all before my parents found out.

One book caught my eye and appeared to be part of a series called Luck in the Shadows. I saw my teacher Mr. Yamata reading it one day and had been meaning to check it out. I grabbed the first three books in the series and turned to Kate.

"See anything you like?" I asked.

She shrugged. "Not yet, but I know there's got to be something."

I nodded. "Yeah, I mean, they have everything."

As she looked through the books, I bit my lip. I still hadn't brought up the comment she had made earlier this week, although it felt it had been a long time since it happened. I had been through a lot with Morpheus and all that, not to mention I had gone to Wonderland

and stayed the night. And almost died. Again.

"Hey, you don't dislike Malcolm, do you?" I asked.

She looked a little shocked I asked, then shook her head. "No, I think he's pretty awesome."

"Then what did you mean earlier this week about I had nothing going for me because I was spending time with him?"

"That wasn't what I meant. I am just saying you have been busy this past year. And pretty soon your parents will find out that you have a boyfriend."

I sighed. "Yeah, I know. It's just complicated. I have been doing better at school, so I don't think it will be an issue. But you know how they get."

"It's just going to be worse when they find out. Especially when you are always together."

There it was again.

"See, that wording makes me feel you don't like me hanging out with him."

"I just think you spend too much time together. It seems like you guys are always hanging out at school and after school when you aren't at dance."

I couldn't believe what I was hearing. We had been dating for a while, not to mention before that we had been together a lot because of things going on in Wonderland. It wasn't my fault that I couldn't explain what was really going on. "Are you jealous?"

"No, I just worry if you two break up that you won't know what to do with yourself. I have seen some other girls fall apart because their boyfriend took all their attention."

"I… I don't spend all my time with him. I have art and dance and…" No, she had a point. But it wasn't just because we were dating—it was because of Morpheus and all the other stuff in Wonderland.

"Look, I meant nothing by it. I just worry for you. But you are right; you two are fine. You are happy and have a lot of other things going on." She grabbed a book off the shelf and smiled. "Should we check out? I'm sure my mom is ready to get some dinner."

I nodded, and we went to check out. As I expected, I had enough credit to cover both our purchases. Score.

We played a round of mini golf and had dinner at the Best Little Roadhouse. My favorite meal there was the tequila pasta. It had a unique flavor that I had never found elsewhere. I took out the peppers though, as I wasn't a fan of their taste or texture.

Once we obtained our cake and headed back to Kate's place, we all finally decided on a movie. None of us had seen *Knives Out* yet, and since we loved a good mystery and comedy, it was an excellent choice.

I took a bite of my raspberry-lemonade cake and relished it with delight. It was my favorite flavor, hands down. I wished all cake tasted this good. It was nice to do all my favorite things with Kate, and I hoped our friendship would last forever.

We were still sophomores, so we had a couple of years before we graduated. I didn't know where I wanted to go to college, but I knew I would have to decide soon. Chemeketa Community College gave free tuition for the first two years to those in the district who had a GPA of 3.5 or higher, but I didn't want to stick around here. I wasn't sure if I even wanted to go to a normal college or a specialized school for art. There were so many choices.

"What are you thinking about?" Kate whispered.

I shrugged. "Just wondering what to do after graduation, where to go, all that."

She patted my arm. "We have a bit. It's not something you need to worry about yet."

I gave her a little thankful smile but realized it was something I had to think about. What was my future? What about my friendships? If we moved to different locations, what was I going to do?

And what about Wonderland?

Chapter 7

All I could see was darkness.

I had no idea where I was, and I did not understand how to get out of here. I was afraid to move as I didn't want to step off a cliff or run into something.

"Is anyone there?" I called out. There was no response.

I felt a slight breeze embrace my skin. It was neither hot nor cold but a perfect temperature. Where was I? And what caused me to come here?

Then it hit me—this was another dream. Morpheus had gotten inside my head again.

"Morpheus!" I called out. "I know you are here! Tell me what you want."

"What I want?" His voice was crisp and dark. He was no longer playing around like he had been the other nights. "I want to destroy the protectors of Wonderland."

"Protectors of Wonderland? What do you mean?" I glanced all around, trying to see if I could find any trace of him, but all I saw was darkness.

"Your boyfriend Malcolm of course. Him and Melvin and Davis. They all deserve to die. Along with you."

"It isn't our fault you were stopped. You were trying to destroy Wonderland and eventually the mortal realm!"

"Why is the mortal realm so important, hmm? Because our dear Alice is from there? It's not like you humans have done anything for us."

"The two worlds are connected. The citizens of Wonderland are the dreams of the people on Earth. So, in fact, if it weren't for my world, then yours would never exist."

"Is that so?" He paused, as if letting the words linger for a moment. "Then why does your world give up on their dreams and cause the death of our citizens?"

I hadn't thought about it that way. "I... Because they don't know."

"And what if they did? What if they knew that they were killing citizens of Wonderland? Do you think your world would change?"

I bit my lip. The fact was, I really doubted anything in my world would change. People would give up on dreams and try to forget about Wonderland, if they even believed it existed.

"That's what I thought. So why was it wrong for me to destroy the dreams before they had to face the harsh reality of humans giving up on their own? I was doing a service."

"No, you had no right. That sort of connection is between the humans and the Wonderland citizens. You shouldn't get to choose when they die."

Suddenly Morpheus was right in front of me. His worn face was barely visible, but I could feel his icy glare. "And neither should your people."

He pushed me back, and I felt as if I were falling down and down and down.

"Alice, wake up!"

My eyes opened to find Kate shaking me. We were in her bedroom. That was right. I had spent the night, and we stayed up late, watching *Parks and Recreation* again. I glanced out the window and saw it was daylight.

"What time is it?" I asked with a yawn.

"It's just past seven. But you were having a nightmare and thrashing about. Are you okay?"

So the dream could affect this world too. I would have to tell Bill and Malcolm. "Yeah, I'm fine. I'm sorry I scared you."

"It must have been some dream to cause such a reaction."

I shrugged. "I don't know. Lately I have been having a repetitive nightmare."

"It's probably from stress. You should try meditating or something."

I closed my eyes. "Yeah, maybe I should."

After we finished our homework, I convinced Mrs. B to drop me off at the mall on Lancaster, which was way inferior to the one downtown. It used to be called the Lancaster Mall, but they changed it to Willamette Town Center. We still called it the Lancaster Mall.

I told Mrs. B my parents were already there shopping for some new racquetball shoes for my sister, but really it was so I could go find Malcolm. I had texted him about the dream, and he wanted to meet up with me so we could go over a plan of action. I wasn't sure what exactly that could be, but I wouldn't say no to seeing him.

Mrs. B dropped me off, and I found Malcolm and Kenny in line for an Orange Julius. I quickly hugged Malcolm and gave him a kiss.

"Awwww how sweet." Kenny looked at us through his heart-shaped hands.

Malcolm shot him a look, but it didn't faze Kenny. I blushed a little and let Malcolm wrap his arms around my waist.

"Want anything?" he asked.

"Well, if you insist, I will take an Orange Julius."

He laughed. "So predictable."

"What? It's called Orange Julius; what else am I

going to order?"

"Says the person who orders chicken strips at *Burger King*."

I stuck my tongue out at him as he ordered. I thanked him, and we grabbed a seat as the others brought over their fast food. Chase and Bill got hot pretzels, and Melvin and Davis ended up getting ice cream from Baskin Robbins.

"So." Bill took a bite of his pretzel. "Tell me about the dream."

I shrugged. "It was in a different spot again. This time it was just blackness and I couldn't see anything except when Morpheus stepped up to talk to me. He did his usual threatening and said that he wanted pretty much everyone at this table dead."

"Even me?" Kenny asked.

I nodded. "I presume so. He didn't say everyone's name exactly, but he did say the protectors of Wonderland."

"What's his motive?" Melvin questioned. "I mean, every villain needs a motive, doesn't he? Why does he want to destroy us so badly?"

"It's because the citizens of Wonderland are tied to this realm, but this realm doesn't care about their dreams, and it affects Wonderland. He thinks it's selfish of humans to toss away their dreams so easily, so he wants to destroy them before they have the chance to expire."

"So he wants to be a god." Malcolm took a sip of his strawberry smoothie. "The god of death."

I nodded. "I suppose so."

Davis shook his head. "That is disgusting. Why does he care so much to want to end their lives like that? It makes no sense."

I shrugged. "I mean, it isn't fair that people in this realm dictate if the citizens of Wonderland live or die. They should be able to live life to the fullest."

"Unless it is the opposite," Malcolm commented. "Something happens to them in Wonderland, and it affects this world. Just like what Morpheus was doing."

I bit my lip. Was that possible? Were dreams here given up simply because a citizen in Wonderland had passed away?

"Even so," Melvin began, "it has been part of Wonderland for a very long time, not to mention time in Wonderland moves differently. Most of the citizens live long lives before anything happens. Why is he doing this now?"

"If that's the case…" I took a sip of my drink. "Then what are you all? What about the king and queen? Are you dreams?"

Malcolm shook his head. "No. Not all the people in Wonderland are dreams. Those who protect and rule are tied to Wonderland but not to anything in this world. We are its protectors, just like Morpheus said."

I tapped the side of my drink with my fingers. "Then what is Morpheus? I mean, he isn't exactly a protector. Is he also a dream?"

"That's what we have been trying to find out." Bill shifted in his chair. "He was never seen in Wonderland before. My guess is he randomly materialized like we all did, although it has been centuries since a new guardian appeared. I think once we figure that out, it will reveal the mystery of his intentions."

"He could have been a dream and somehow became something more," Malcolm added. "Anything is possible in Wonderland."

"That it is." Kenny clapped his hands. "Like all of us coming together and eating pretzels and ice cream and smoothies! Here, in this wonderful... What's it called again?"

"A mall," I answered.

"Mall. That is fun to say. Mall."

Bill coughed. "Tonight I will keep surveillance around your house. If he is using a portal, I will find out."

I nodded. "That sounds like a plan. Just keep an eye out for Mr. Petrovitsky. He doesn't like trespassers."

"I will be stealthy. Which means Kenny will not be there."

Kenny pouted. "But I love going on missions with you."

"But you are loud and obnoxious."

"Well, fine. I'll just stay up all night, eating the cookies and candy you think you hid well enough from me. Fun fact, you didn't. I know which cupboard they are in."

I laughed. Sitting together like this made me happy I stumbled upon Wonderland. But deep in my heart, I knew it couldn't last. It was only a matter of time before it all fell apart and shattered like a mirror. I just hoped it wouldn't be for a while.

"Did you finish all your homework?" my mom asked as I started to retire for the night after prepping the food for the big dish I was bringing everyone for lunch tomorrow. I decided to make mexican street corn nachos. Who didn't like nachos? That way I just needed to bring the toppings and some chips and we would be set.

"Yes, Mom. I'm going to paint for a bit and then go to bed."

"Good night, dear."

I opened a door and held back a scream. "What the —?"

Malcolm put his finger to his lips.

"What is it, Meredith?" My mom used my real name. I hated that.

"Nothing. I just forgot how much of a mess I left it in. I'll clean it up tonight."

As quickly as I could, I stepped in my room and shut the door.

"What are you doing here? You are going to get caught."

Malcolm shook his head. "Don't worry about that. I wanted to watch over you to make sure Morpheus doesn't get to you."

I sat down on my bed. "I thought Bill was making sure Morpheus doesn't make a portal."

He settled next to me and traced his knuckles on my arm. "We aren't sure if that is how he is getting in your dreams. I want to be next to you. I can't stand the thought of you fighting him alone like this."

I blushed. Leaning in, I kissed him on the cheek. "Thank you."

"My pleasure. So, what are you going to paint tonight?"

Glancing around, I shrugged. "I don't know. What do you think?"

"How about a cat?" a voice said from the closet.

I jumped up. "Chase?"

"Shh, not so loud." He put his finger to his lips. "Don't want your family to come in here."

Suddenly my door creaked open. It was my sister, Lilith. "What the heck is going on in here?"

"I can explain!" I yelled. "I—"

"I thought I heard you scream. Why are you screaming?" She folded her arms.

Malcolm whispered, "She doesn't see me, and Chase is already gone."

I glanced over to see Chase had in fact disappeared. "Uh, I stubbed my toe really hard."

She rolled her eyes. "You are so clumsy for someone who does ballet. I bet you actually suck at it."

I stuck out my tongue at her as she closed the door. Suddenly Chase reappeared.

"That was close," Chase whispered.

I turned to Malcolm. "How come she couldn't see you?"

He sighed. "I have the power of illusion. It's technically illegal for me to use it in Wonderland."

"Because you misused it plenty of times," Chase added. "And you would actually be hanged if you got caught."

"But we aren't in Wonderland, so it's fine."

I guess that made sense. There was still a lot I didn't quite understand about him. He was a mystery even though we had been a couple for a few months now.

Taking a deep breath, I grabbed some watercolor paper.

"I guess I could paint a cat."

Chase grinned at Malcolm, who just turned away from him.

"What are you even doing here, cat?"

"Protecting Alice, what does it look like?"

"You should be back with the others. I can handle

this on my own."

Chase put his hands on his waist. "I'm not leaving you alone with Alice. That would be like leaving Alice with a wolf."

"I already told you, I am a gentleman, unlike you."

I held up my hand. "Stop fighting. Someone will hear you. Chase, you can stay. I would feel better if more than one person was with me tonight."

Malcolm frowned, but I knew he understood. There was safety in numbers. I grabbed my watercolor palate. "Now, what color should I make this cat?"

Chapter 8

"You think they can protect you?" Morpheus whispered in my ear. "You think just because they are in your room that it will stop me?"

Darkness surrounded me once again. This time I was not afraid—this time I knew it was a dream and that he couldn't hurt me with Chase and Malcolm nearby.

I nodded. "They are my friends. We are all in this together to defeat you."

"Silly girl, you are alone. They keep secrets from you. They lie to you. You don't even know their past."

"I know they are good people."

He laughed. "Oh really, then maybe you should ask Malcolm what happened to him in the Dark Forest."

"Alice!" I heard a voice call. "Wake up, Alice!"

My eyes flickered open to find Malcolm and Chase

hovering over me. Their eyes were wide as they looked down at me. Malcolm let out a sigh of relief.

"Alice, you were having another nightmare. Was it Morpheus?" Chase asked.

I nodded. "Yeah."

"What happened?" Malcolm stroked my hand with his thumb.

"I… I don't know. It was all darkness, and he was trying to tell me I was alone."

Malcolm sat down next to me on the bed. "You are not alone. I will never leave you, Alice. I will always be here to protect you."

Chase stared at Malcolm, and I didn't know what he was thinking. He appeared almost jealous.

I sat up in my bed. "Thank you. I just don't know what to do. I'm afraid to go to sleep."

"Here, lay your head on my lap. Then you will know I am here when you wake up."

I blushed and slowly laid my head on his lap. It was strange, but it felt comfortable. I could feel his heat, and it helped calm me down.

Within a few moments, I fell back asleep.

Malcolm and Chase disappeared before my parents were up, and I finished making the nachos to bring to school. They, of course, were a hit. I couldn't help eating more than my share as they were one of my favorite snacks.

The rest of the day and Tuesday went by as normal as it could with Malcolm and Chase spending the night. I felt secure when they were around but worried constantly that my parents or sister would walk in at any given moment. Malcolm said he could make it so they didn't see him, but Chase had to transport out of there. And what if they were asleep and my family walked in? I couldn't even imagine their reaction. It was a wonder I could sleep at all.

Most of the dreams I had were the same as the past two in that I could only see darkness instead of a particular place in Wonderland. Bill didn't find any trace of Morpheus around my house, so whatever he was doing had nothing to do with portals. That part of the trail was a dead end.

It was Wednesday now, and as I did every Wednesday, I had dance class after school. I grabbed my bike and started walking toward the entrance of the school when I heard Chase calling after me.

"Alice!"

I turned to find him running across the grass. "What is it?"

"Are you sure you are fine riding your bike to class? You haven't been sleeping well, and I saw you start to doze off during US History. I don't want you falling while you bike and get in an accident."

He had a point; I had been tired these past few days.

"Are you up for transporting us? Are you sure no

one will notice?"

Chase nodded. "I'm sure. I've done it many times now. There are plenty of areas around there that are abandoned this time of day. Just leave it to me."

"Fine. But where are we going to transport from on this end?"

"The shop class is usually closed up by now, and it's an easy doorway to go through with no one noticing."

I sighed. It was on the opposite side of campus. "Lead the way."

We walked back toward campus and headed to the shop. I didn't take shop, although I wanted to my junior or senior year. I thought it would be fun to work with wood as it was a medium I hadn't used yet. We had a lot of different electives available, mainly in our junior and senior year, and I was excited to try some. I would have to narrow it down sooner or later, as there was no way I could fit it all in my schedule.

Especially since I would be forced to take AP classes.

As we went around the first building, I ran into my sister Lilith as she was walking to her car. Crap.

"Meredith, what are you doing back here? Aren't you heading to dance class?" she asked as she glanced at Chase. "Who's this?"

Crap, she was totally going to tell my parents I was going toward a secluded area of school after I was supposed to be biking to dance.

"He's just a friend. We have dance together, and he

forgot something in shop class."

She raised an eyebrow. "He does dance? He doesn't happen to be the boy that got you into detention, does he?"

Crap times infinity.

"So what if I am?" Chase stepped forward. "What are you going to do about it?"

"Chase, no…"

Lilith tossed her long brown hair back and laughed. "You are in so much trouble tonight. I can't wait for dinnertime."

With that, she left us standing there. I pinched the bridge of my nose.

"Your sister seems like a stuck-up b—"

"I know, but I also know that wasn't an empty threat. I am in so much trouble."

Chase frowned. "I'm sorry I caused you trouble, Alice. I didn't mean to…"

I held up my hand. "It's fine. I'll figure it out later. Let's just get to class."

Chase and I headed toward the shop class, and after double-checking to make sure the coast was clear, Chase teleported into one of the abandoned warehouses near the dance studio. One of the homeless men from the Union Gospel Mission ran away when he saw us suddenly appear. Oops.

"He will have a wonderful story to tell his friends. Anyway, we should hurry so we can change."

I nodded and walked my bike toward the dance studio.

"Oh, Alice, you must have gotten out early. Usually you are never here before 3:15," Becca said as we came in.

Right. I forgot to take time into consideration. I checked the clock and saw it was 3:05.

"Uh, yeah… We had an assembly." Luckily there weren't any other students from East Salem High who took dance, so the only person who could reveal my lie was Chase, but since he was in on the lie, that didn't seem likely.

"It was really boring," Chase added.

We hurried off to change and get ready for warm-ups. I tried not to think about what was waiting for me at home. My mom and dad were going to be pissed. What was I going to tell them? That I had lied? And there was also the fact that Chase took dance with me. Were they going to make me stop taking dance? I knew they would try to threaten, but I had kept my grades up and I hadn't gotten in any more trouble. They just didn't understand.

The thought about running away to Wonderland and never coming back crossed my mind. I couldn't actually do that as I had a lot going on here. I had Kate and… anime?

Ah. I saw what Kate was trying to tell me now.

Something in my chest started to feel heavy as I

realized I would need to eventually make a choice between the two worlds. I couldn't juggle both my entire life. But I knew I had a while before that would happen. At least that was what I hoped.

As we started practicing pirouettes again, I noticed something in the entry to the dance studio. I saw the figure of a scruffy man wearing a tattered jacket and a dusty top hat.

Morpheus.

Suddenly everything started spinning around me and it all went black.

"Alice! Wake up! Alice!"

I opened my eyes to find Chase's face flushed and his eyes almost red with tears. I blinked a few times and felt as if something had hit my head. Glancing around, I realized I was still at dance.

"What happened?"

Becca knelt down next to me. "You passed out. I called a medic and your parents already, and they are on their way."

I shook my head. "No ambulances, please."

"You need to be checked out. You literally just collapsed. They won't take you to the hospital if you don't need it."

This was so embarrassing. Everyone was staring at me as I lay there. I tried to get up, but my head was still pounding. Chase quickly helped me as I stumbled.

"Sit over here while you wait for the medic." Becca ushered me over to a bench.

I nodded and Chase sat down next to me.

"Do you need anything else?" Becca asked.

I shook my head.

"Okay, I will talk with the class on what they need to work on next, and I will be right back."

As she walked away, Chase leaned in to whisper, "What happened?"

"I saw Morpheus and then I completely blacked out. Chase, I don't know what's going on. He seems to be everywhere. What should I do?"

He frowned and shook his head. "I don't know. But we will figure it out. I won't let any harm come to you."

I smiled as I felt reassured. Although he was a goofball, he was a good friend and ally. I was glad to have him on my side.

After getting checked out and cleared by the medic, my parents took me home. I knew I would see Chase later that night, as I doubted he and Malcolm would leave me alone tonight. After Lilith seeing us enter and my parents quickly telling her about my fall, she held her mouth about bumping into Chase and me. I didn't know if it was because she was going to bring it up later or if she was going to blackmail me. Either way, it was just another worry on top of everything else.

Dinner came and went, and I retired early for the night. My head still hurt, and even though I needed to prep lunch, I decided tomorrow would be cafeteria food. I was sure Malcolm would understand, especially since I could tell him the moment I went into my room.

Sure enough, Malcolm was already there with Chase sitting on my desk chair.

"Tell me everything that happened," Malcolm said as he embraced me.

I shrugged. "It's the same as usual. I saw him and then completely blacked out."

"Did he say anything?"

I shook my head. "No. I just saw him in the doorway and everything spun around me and I collapsed."

"This isn't good. Bill checked it out after you left, and there is no way he transported here."

"So what you are saying is that either Bill is mistaken or I am seeing things."

"You aren't seeing things."

"Well, I mean, I didn't see Morpheus at class."

We both turned to Chase.

"What do you mean?" Malcolm asked.

"I mean I was at dance and saw nothing in the doorway. I was looking that way when Alice collapsed. So I don't think he is physically here. I think he is in Alice's mind."

I sat on the bed and held my head in my hands. "Ugh, this is just swell. I'm going crazy."

Malcolm shook his head. "No, he is affecting you somehow. You aren't crazy. We will figure it out. I promise."

I wrapped my arms around him. "Thank you. And by the way, we have to eat in the cafeteria tomorrow."

He laughed. "That's fine." He kissed my forehead. "Now, did you remember to do geometry homework?"

I collapsed on my bed and fake wept. That was something I did not want to be doing at the moment, especially with such a pounding headache.

"Do you think Kate will help me do it at lunch tomorrow?"

Malcolm stroked my back. "How about I do it, you can copy it, then tomorrow I will go over what I did to make sure you understand it."

"That sounds like a good idea. Thank you."

"Can I copy yours too?" Chase asked.

Malcolm glared at him. "No."

Chase collapsed on my beanbag chair. "Ugh."

There was a knock on my door, and my mom walked in. She didn't notice Malcolm, and Chase somehow was able to disappear in time. She held out her hand. "Here is some Motrin for the headache. Do you need anything else?"

I shook my head. "No, thanks, Mom."

She smiled and left. I took the Motrin and watched as Chase reappeared.

He sighed. "That was close."

"You better be on guard. She probably will check up on me before she goes to bed."

"Speaking of, I think you need to go to sleep. You haven't slept well all week," Malcolm said as he helped tuck me in.

"Yeah, well, that's not my fault."

"True. Hopefully he doesn't come back."

I sighed. One could always hope, couldn't they?

Chapter 9

The night went by, and even though I didn't want to sleep, I passed out the moment I laid my head on my pillow. I didn't dream of Morpheus again, which I was thankful for, and when I woke up, my headache was gone. I had nothing prepped though, so I didn't have time to make a bento for Malcolm. I knew he understood, but I felt kind of bad as he had been staying with me every night. I owed him.

I also owed the Duchess and needed to think of something to make for her to show my thanks. If it weren't for her, I would have been dead right now. It was definitely not something I liked thinking about.

But I needed to defeat Morpheus to really be in the clear.

I got ready and made my way to school with my

sister. As we got in the car, she turned to me.

"I was thinking. I hate doing the dishes and laundry and cleaning my room, and I have a lot of dirt on you."

I sighed. "Whatever. I don't trust you enough to believe you would hold up your end of the bargain if I did your chores. And how long would it even go on for? You could just keep holding it over me until you graduate. That's a lot of chores."

She placed her finger on her chin. "Wow, you can actually think about the future. I am rather surprised."

"Yeah, well? What deal are you going to make me?"

"Hmm… How about for a month you do my chores, clean my room, and make me lunch?"

I sighed. "Fine. But if you tell Mom and Dad, I will sneak into your room and shave off all your hair."

"And I will destroy all your art."

"And we would just keep going until one of us is kicked out."

"Which would be you."

That was fair. It probably would be me. "I'm just saying, do we have ourselves a deal?"

"I suppose. But I have to ask, are you two dating?"

I shook my head. "No, we are just friends."

"That's what I figured. No boy in their right mind would date you."

I stuck my tongue out at her as she started the car, and we headed toward the school. The giant painted owl on the concrete entrance greeted us as we hurried off in our opposite directions. Most of the upperclassmen were in the complete opposite building as those for freshman and sophomores, which is what made it easy for me to hide that Malcolm and I were dating. It wasn't like rumors about me circled around, not to mention not many cared about me. I was invisible.

I kept my fingers crossed that it would stay that way. Otherwise, I was going to be in a lot of trouble. At least I could always run away to Wonderland. For now.

I got to English and sat behind Chase. It had been a few days, but I kept forgetting Kenny was "teaching" this class. He did not know much about literature, so it was pretty entertaining. Mr. Barnes was getting more and more frustrated each and every day. I loved it, as did many in my class. It made me wonder if that was why Malcolm had him be the English student teacher —to piss off Mr. Barnes.

"Today we will discuss more about what the meaning is behind *1984* before starting our next unit next week, which is…" Kenny turned to Mr. Barnes.

"*Huckleberry Finn.*"

"Oh, I do love berries. Will there be a tart?"

Again with the tarts. He really seemed to fixate on them. I wished I could have been there the first time when there was the trial. Then again, maybe I didn't want to meet the Queen of Hearts.

Mr. Barnes just stared at him as if he were crazy.

"No."

Kenny pouted as he went on with class. He didn't seem to be getting the hang of it all, however, and I had a feeling he read all of *1984* this past weekend. That or someone showed him SparkNotes.

Morning classes went by as normal, other than Kate had a meeting with her track group during lunch. I was lucky Malcolm helped me with homework. We were able to go over it quickly, and I felt I understood it all. That was a first.

I was seeing much less of Kate each and every day, but I was glad she was doing so well in her sport. As for lunch itself, the cafeteria served nothing spectacular, so I had some pizza. It tasted like cardboard, which was exactly what I expected. Malcolm got some chicken nuggets and fries, but he just picked at them, so I had a feeling they weren't that great. Next year we would be able to eat off campus, and I was excited as there was a Taco Time nearby. And Chipotle.

Maybe I could get my sister to stop there after school and we could get a late-lunch-early-dinner snack. It wasn't like it would spoil my appetite as I was always hungry.

I couldn't wait for the day to be over so I could get some more rest because tomorrow we had a field trip to the Oregon Zoo. It had been a long time since I had visited, and they had opened a lot of different exhibits.

I always enjoyed seeing the adorable penguins. They were like animals in little suits.

"So, are you all ready for the zoo trip tomorrow?" I asked as Melvin and Davis took their seats. All five of us were at the table now.

Chase shrugged. "What's so cool about seeing a bunch of animals stuck in cages?"

Davis's eyes widened. "They are in cages? Those poor creatures!"

"They aren't in cages per se, more like big exhibits. And most, if not all, grew up in captivity or were saved from dying in the wild. They wouldn't be able to go back into the wild and survive. So zoos are keeping those animals safe," I explained.

Davis let out a sigh of relief. "Oh, okay. I guess that makes sense."

"Just don't fall into the tiger exhibit, Davis," Chase added. "That big cat will probably be able to tell you are a mouse."

"That's not funny!"

Chase laughed as he finished up his tuna salad sandwich. The rest of lunch was much the same, mainly Chase naming all the ways Davis could get eaten on the zoo trip. No matter what he said though, I was looking forward to it and hoped that we would be in the same group. They had never been inside a zoo, and I wanted to witness their reaction to everything. Especially the tropical bird exhibit that you could walk around in.

I prayed Chase wouldn't come out of there with a bird in his mouth, just like a cat would. I shook the image out of my mind as I threw away the rest of my pizza into the compost. Hopefully my stomach wouldn't growl the entire class time.

Math came and went, and after changing for PE, I met up with Malcolm. It was our turn to get the supplies from the closet since today we were playing flag football. As we opened up the supply closet, I gasped in surprise. There, in the closet, were Bill and Kenny with their lips pressed firmly together and arms wrapped around each other. I put my hand over my mouth, surprised to find the two of them making out.

Actually, to be honest, I wasn't. That was just a matter of time.

Bill blushed. "Oh, is it time for class already?"

Malcolm nodded. "Yup. Flag football today. You are lucky we were the ones who found you."

Kenny clapped his hands. "Well, I'm also late for class, so I will see you all later." He turned to Bill. "And definitely you later."

Bill winked at him as Kenny ran off toward his classroom. Turning to us, Bill smiled. "Okay, so help me find the things we need for this flag football."

We grabbed all the stuff we needed for PE and

headed back into the gym. Everyone was stretching, warming up, or chatting away with their friends. It was a mad dash of who wanted what color, and I ended up being on the opposite side of Malcolm and Melvin, but Chase and Davis were on my side, as was Kate.

Chase patted my back. "Don't worry, Alice, we are going to defeat your boyfriend and make him realize we are the best at this game."

"Do you even know how to play flag football?"

"It doesn't matter; we will win."

I let out a sigh. It was going to be an interesting class, I could already tell.

After we'd finished our stretches and Bill finished reading from a manual on how to play, we all settled in the grass. A couple of students set up the boundaries and goals while Bill got ready for the coin toss. It was heads, so Malcolm's team got to start.

I had to hand it to Chase—he was able to pick up the game quickly. I expected him to either cheat or actually tackle Malcolm or Melvin when they had the ball, but he didn't. Davis, on the other hand, was rather scared for the most part. He was fast though and could run past everyone out of sheer terror. He scored us a couple of touchdowns.

The ball was in my hands, and I tried to run for a touchdown, but Malcolm was on the way. He, technically, was only supposed to grab the flags on my belt, but instead he wrapped his arms around me.

"Hey! That's not fair!" I said.

"Too bad, too sad. Bill isn't looking, and I'm going to get away with it."

Glancing around, I saw Kate was open. I quickly threw it to her, and she was able to move past everyone and score a touchdown. She definitely knew how to run. I turned to face Malcolm and stuck my tongue out.

"I guess my plans were foiled. Oh well."

Bill ran over, blowing his whistle. "Foul! Malcolm, you are out."

Malcolm nodded toward the bell tower. "It doesn't matter. The period is over in five minutes."

Bill looked at the clock. "I guess you are right. Well then, team B is the winner! Now everyone put everything away. And don't forget, tomorrow is the sophomore trip up to the Oregon Zoo! I will be one of your chaperones, so get ready for a day of fun!"

"Oh God," I commented. "Don't tell me Kenny is also a chaperone."

Malcolm nodded. "Yup."

I let out a sigh. "Well, then tomorrow will be a day to remember."

Chapter 10

It was way too early to be on a bus.

I yawned as I leaned my head on Malcolm's shoulder, watching as we passed by Woodburn Outlet Mall. I needed to remember to pick up some new Converse at the Converse store this weekend as mine were starting to get worn on the bottom. And perhaps get a cinnamon roll at Cinnabon and try to eat it all in one sitting, if that was even possible.

"You are not a morning person, are you?" Malcolm said as he adjusted in his seat.

"I hate mornings so much," I moaned. "And it doesn't help that I always have those nightmares."

"Last night you seemed fine though."

"Yeah, but it still has affected most of my week. I think this weekend I am going to just sleep the entire time."

Malcolm grabbed my hand and stroked the top with his thumb. "I thought you wanted to go out on a date."

I sighed. "How about we go to Wonderland then? I can just sleep for a few days, come back, and it will only be a few minutes or hours or whatever it decides this time, and then we can have our date."

He laughed. "That sounds like a good plan."

Chase, who was sitting in front of us, turned around in his seat. "What we really need to do is go to Wonderland and find Morpheus. I have a feeling he is somewhere in the Dark Forest and we just missed him."

Malcolm shook his head. "There is no way he is in the Dark Forest. I didn't find any trace of him."

"And you are capable of looking everywhere in the Dark Forest?"

"Yes."

Chase frowned. "Well, either way, I thought the plan was for us to head back and take a look around. Hopefully we find something and we can end this once and for all."

Malcolm nodded. "That is the plan. But that doesn't mean Alice and I can't go on that date."

Chase rolled his eyes and turned back around. He did have a point however, as we needed to figure out where Morpheus was and stop him. I still wasn't sure why he would only affect me or target me when there wasn't much I could do in Wonderland.

However, he kept saying I could change Wonderland with my power.

What did that even mean? I figured it was because I was able to stop him, but besides that, what about Wonderland could be changed? Everything was great other than the chaos he made. I had spent a year traveling all through the land, and I saw nothing but peace and tranquility.

So why did he want to mess that up?

I thought back on how he was mad about my world, killing or destroying the dreams that resided in Wonderland. I pondered on how he thought it was better to control them and kill them himself. What was his purpose? Everything in Wonderland had a purpose —everything materialized for a reason. What was his? Was it just to throw a wrench in things, like the Queen of Hearts? Or was there more to it when it came to the dreams in general? I felt there were pieces of the story that I didn't have yet.

We traveled on the bus for over an hour until we reached the entrance to the Oregon Zoo, passing Uwajimaya on the way, which made me sad as I really wanted to stop by there. That wasn't going to happen while on this bus trip, but maybe later this weekend.

There were already a lot of people lined up to get into the zoo, along with students of all ages from other schools. It always seemed like more than one school would take a field trip to the zoo. The bus dropped us off at the front gate, and our chaperone, Bill, raised a bright green piece of paper.

"We will be splitting into groups! Malcolm, Melvin, Davis, Chase, and Alice, you are with Mr. Knave and me!" He went on to separate everyone else into groups with their designated chaperone.

Yeah, he totally rearranged the groups so we would all be together. It was obvious, and I heard some of the other students whispering about being favorites. Whatever. I wasn't going to complain, especially since all of them hadn't been to a zoo before. And I got to be with my friends.

I turned to Kate. "Hope you have fun in your group. Eat lunch together? I think we all have lunch break at the same time."

She nodded as she glanced at my group. "Yeah, that sounds good."

Our group waited for Bill to finish giving the details to everyone. Apparently after lunch we had the option of going over to the Rose Garden or having free time around the zoo.

"Ooh, a rose garden?" Kenny commented from behind us. "Do you think there is a queen there?"

Davis turned to him. "Shhh, Mr. L is still talking."

"He always talks. I don't get why we need to listen; he's coming with us."

Chase sighed. "This is going to be a long day."

"What's that supposed to mean?"

Chase glanced over at Kenny. "You are a bit much ninety percent of the time."

Kenny smiled. "Why, thank you."

"That wasn't a compliment."

Suddenly a half-empty water bottle came flying at the group and smacked Kenny straight in the face. I gasped.

Kenny rubbed his nose and looked over at Bill. "Hey, what was that for?"

Bill smiled. "Don't talk while I'm talking." Bill clapped his hands. "Well, that's it, everyone. Have fun and stay safe."

The groups went to their different sections of the zoo. Our group was to start at the Pacific Northwest. The mountain goats awaited all attendees, settled between the front restaurant, ticket stand, and gift shop.

"Oh, look at them!" Kenny exclaimed, jumping up and down, causing other zoo attendees and volunteers to stare at us. "How can they stand like that? It's adorable!"

Bill patted him on the back. "It's okay, Kenny. They are just goats. You've seen goats."

"But these have beards! Look at them!"

I held back a laugh. Kenny was going to lose it at every exhibit, I could already tell. I had to agree though, these goats looked funny with the beards, and it was amazing they could climb such steep mountains.

Once we were able to pull Kenny away from the goats, we made it down the path toward the rest of the exhibits to find black bears below us.

"What are those?" Melvin asked, a little nervous.

"Black bears. They are very big and very scary to come across. My relatives in Washington have seen them in their yard."

All of them looked at me with such terror. Melvin asked, "They walk around in the wild here?"

I nodded slowly. "Yes, everything in this section is somewhere in the wild around here."

They all looked back down at the bears as if it was the scariest thing they had ever seen. It made me laugh a little. They had trisings that nearly killed them, giant spiders, a magical circus that nearly destroyed everyone, and a Jabberwocky, but this was somehow scarier.

We checked out the fish and birds, including a couple of bald eagles. Chase, throughout the entire walk, had huge, hungry eyes. He definitely reacted like a cat. Little did he realize that some of these birds would probably win in a fight against him.

Coming upon the cougars, Davis let out a high-pitched sound. "Eeep!"

Everyone turned around as Chase put his hand on Davis's mouth. He leaned in and whispered, "Look, little mouse, a big kitty!"

Davis shook his head as Chase pushed him toward the netting. The cougar was pacing right in front of the viewing area. Poor Davis looked like he wanted to cry.

"Please don't…," Davis whispered.

"He can't hurt you. There's netting in the way."

"But he's staring at me like he wants to eat me!"

"You are just mistaken. He just wants to play!"

Bill placed his hand on Chase's shoulder. "That's enough. Leave the poor mouse alone."

Chase let go of Davis, and Davis ran over to me with tears in his eyes. "Alice, he's being mean!"

I patted him on the head. "There, there. It's okay now. Let's go look at the other exhibits."

We made our way to the next section, which included animals from the Pacific shore, so mainly seals, otters, and penguins. The moment we stepped into the fishy-smelling building, Chase took in a deep breath.

"It smells great in here!"

I wrinkled my nose. "No, it really doesn't."

The rest of us nodded. The smell was almost overpowering, but I supposed this area would smell fishy with the animals they needed to feed, and the fact it's sort of what the beach smelled like. Maybe just a little stronger.

Chase sighed. "I'm starving. When is lunch?"

Bill checked his watch. "In a little over an hour. Eat a snack if you are hungry."

Chase glanced over at the fish.

"Not those, for the love of Wonderland."

I nodded at the elephant ears stand. "We could get an elephant ear."

Chase raised an eyebrow. "No to fish, but it's okay to eat an elephant?"

I shook my head. "No, it's a fried bread with sugar and cinnamon."

Everyone, including Malcolm, seemed to be intrigued. "Where is this and how many can we purchase?"

I led everyone to the stand, and we were able to get it quickly. We bought three and shared them between the four of us. It was sweet, doughy, but had the right amount of crisp to it. It was the best.

"We should bring this to Wonderland! I think it would do very well in the market area," Bill commented.

I nodded. "I can find a recipe online, and we can give it to one of the stalls to make. Maybe they will even give us free ones as a thank-you."

"That would be spectacular." Malcolm took another bite of ours. "I would be forever thankful to you."

I blushed as we headed down toward the chimpanzee exhibit. Soon there was going to be a large primate exhibit, but it wasn't open yet. The chimps weren't that exciting, as they were just lying around when we saw them.

Next was lunch. I was excited, as I was starving, even after sharing that elephant ear. The Africafé was always fun since you could look down at one of the bird exhibits. I went and ordered my animal fries and some chicken strips, as it was always my favorite when going to the zoo. Luckily I remembered to bring cash this time instead of having to borrow from Kate. I spotted Kate and found she had already gotten a table with her group, which was mostly track team members.

"Hey, Kate!" I waved.

"Oh hey! We already got a seat since we got here early. So I am probably just going to hang out here. I'll see you on the bus though. I think our group isn't going to go over to the rose garden though."

I nodded. "Yeah, sure. No worries. I'll see you later!"

I went over and sat with my group. Everyone was laughing about something, and Davis looked down, frowning.

"What is it now?" I asked him.

"They said they are going to throw me in the tiger pit to see what would happen."

I sighed. "Don't worry, they won't. I will be there to make sure you don't get thrown in. As for you, Bill and Kenny, you are supposed to be making sure everyone is fine, not egging them on."

Kenny pouted. "We were just kidding. I wouldn't hurt a fly. Unless it was a nasty fly, then maybe. Or a wasp. Or a trising."

Malcolm shook his head. "I can't believe I talked the school into hiring them."

"How did you manage that, by the way? Usually it's harder than just asking."

"Oh, I used a hypnotic-like power I have."

I just stared at him. "Your what?"

"It's like how I can be at your house without your parents noticing. A power I have but am not technically allowed to use."

"But this is Earth and not Wonderland."

He winked. "Precisely."

"You sure you won't get in trouble?"

He shook his head. "Bill was there, and he would be the one to arrest me if that were the case. He said since it was to catch Morpheus, that it was fine."

"Ah. I guess that is a good reason. I'm just surprised I didn't know about those powers before."

"Hasn't come up. And not many know about it since, well, I'm not allowed to use them." He smiled to me as if he thought it was a bit funny. I sort of smiled back.

I rolled my eyes as I glanced over at Kate. She seemed to be having fun with the other track team members. I guess that was a good thing, but I wasn't used to how much time I was away from her this past year. Now she was moving on, and so was I.

It was rather strange. But I guess I needed to get

used to it, especially if I was going to move to some other state for college. Or maybe even Wonderland.

Chapter 11

Our group finished up lunch and went to check out the birds. Chase had a blast letting them land on him. I could tell he wanted to catch one, but that wasn't allowed. I made sure to remind him of that frequently.

We also made our way through the Africa exhibit and found it to be quite spectacular. It was very well done and huge compared to many of the other exhibits. Davis didn't like the lions… or the tigers…

Once we were done exploring the zoo, we met up with the other groups that wanted to visit the Rose Garden. I figured Malcolm and the others wanted to see the gardens since Wonderland was full of flowers, or maybe they missed the Heart Kingdom's rose garden. Flowers were beautiful, so I didn't blame them.

Kate's group wasn't going over to the Rose Garden,

which was a shame. There were rows upon rows of roses. I hadn't been here since I was little and was flabbergasted by all the beautiful flowers. Pulling out my phone, I took a few pictures so I could paint them later.

Malcolm wrapped his arm around my waist and smiled. "You are so cute when you get a painting idea."

I blushed. "How did you know?"

"Because we've been around each other for a while now. I can tell."

I stuck my tongue out at him. "Well, you are right. Come on, I want to get some close-ups as well."

We walked over to some of the roses that had yellow-and-pink petals. I snapped a few shots and moved on to the dark red roses.

"This place is spectacular! I wish I could live among flowers like this all the time."

Malcolm smiled. "Well, Wonderland has some beautiful gardens that we haven't visited yet. Perhaps we will go visit them sometime."

"Yeah, we should. Wonderland is so beautiful. There doesn't seem to be a part of Wonderland that I don't hate. Well, maybe the Dark Forest, but even then it was a place that would be worthy of painting. I don't think I will ever get bored in Wonderland."

"There's a lot in Wonderland to see. It has to be that way since some of us live for long periods of time. Everything is always changing, so it never gets dull."

"I can't wait to see everything. It inspires me to be there. I wish I could stay there forever."

Malcolm turned to me. "You would want to live there forever?"

I stumbled on my words. "Yeah. I mean, I think if I had a choice, I would pick Wonderland. I have a life there, and the society is more where I would fit in. This world... I don't know... Most of my friends are from Wonderland, and it's not like my family likes what I want to do with my life." I looked up at Malcolm, who had a very stoic face. Did he not like the idea of me picking Wonderland? "I mean... if I had to make a choice. But I know there's more to it than that."

He frowned a little, and when he was about to answer, Chase called over.

"Hey, did you check out these? They are red and white! Imagine the Queen of Hearts if she saw these!"

Malcolm's face changed in an instant. "Let's go see what Chase found."

I nodded, wondering what he was originally going to say to me. I didn't know if I would be brave enough to bring it up. First Kate was trying to say I spent too much time with these guys, and now I felt as if Malcolm was going to say I couldn't choose to stay in Wonderland. I didn't want to imagine a life without Wonderland. I don't think I could ever be happy.

Malcolm led us to where Chase was admiring the roses. The rose appeared white with red spots sprinkled throughout. I pulled out my phone and took a picture.

Bending down to take a better look, Malcolm laughed. "Yeah, she would have freaked."

Kenny and Bill came over. Kenny pointed at the rose and laughed. "Could you imagine the queen seeing that rose! Oh my goodness!"

"We already said that. You're late to the game, Kenny," Chase commented.

Kenny pouted. "But I just got here."

Davis and Melvin joined us to admire the multicolored flower.

"Hey, wouldn't the—?" Melvin began.

"We know," everyone said in unison.

We all started laughing. They had all thought the same thing, and for the most part, I understood why they thought it was so funny. Apparently that part of Lewis Carroll's adaptation was correct.

Kenny shook his head. "Man, I remember having to paint a whole field of roses red. It was not easy. Each day a new bloom would appear, and I would have to go through it all and repaint them."

Malcolm added, "And that's why you had to eat her tarts, right?"

"I was starving! You have any idea how much work it is to paint all those flowers? I was so hungry, and she wasn't going to eat that tart!"

I rolled my eyes. Here we go again. He always liked

going on about that tart. I didn't even know much time had passed technically as time moved differently when we were in Wonderland.

"We were at the trial, Kenny, we know." Chase leaned back and looked up at the sky.

Kenny nudged Malcolm. "And good ol' Malcolm here lied in court for me, didn't ya?"

Malcolm nodded. "I did. That's when Alice came and got me out of the Dark Forest to help you and then help overthrow the kingdom."

"Those were the days." Kenny sighed.

"Back when Malcolm was still the Mad Hatter," Chase commented. "And was feared wherever he went."

Malcolm glared at Chase. He simply shrugged. "Just saying how it was."

"We were all in the Dark Forest," Melvin said. "Including you."

Chase shrugged. "I was just exploring. I wasn't participating in whatever the hell you three were doing."

Davis shoved Chase. "Shut up. No one trusts you because you can't side with anyone except the Duchess!"

Chase rolled his eyes.

"The Duchess?" I asked. She was the one who saved me, but when we ran into her, it didn't seem like Chase really cared about her one way or another, not to mention I hadn't heard anything about her in all the time I was in Wonderland.

"He is that lady's pet." Malcolm glowered at Chase. "The Duchess can order this feline to do whatever she wants, although she is so fickle that it doesn't seem like Chase cares one way or another, does it?"

Chase narrowed his eyes. "I haven't been her pet in a very long time. I am owned by no one."

I had a feeling this fight was going to escalate quickly, and so I clapped my hands. "Well, shall we keep looking around? We don't have too much time before we have to head back to school."

Everyone nodded and mostly went around in their own little groups. I stayed with Malcolm, and we held hands as we ventured around. Chase went off on his own, and I lost sight of him. He would come back before we had to get on the bus, or at least I hoped he would.

I turned to Malcolm. "So what is the story between Chase and the Duchess?"

"He was technically her cat and would do anything ordered. He caused a lot of trouble in her name, and that was why most people don't like him. She sides with whoever she believes has the most power, so the Queen of Hearts, and so on. She doesn't have any loyalty either, so it made Chase seem even worse."

"But if he was ordered and couldn't disobey, why was he held responsible?" I asked.

"Because he goes about things a little more chaotically than most. Don't worry, he is starting to get more and more accepted as times goes on, unfortunately."

"Poor Chase."

"Why do you care? He is a troublemaker and you know that. He got you in detention, didn't he? Now imagine him being like that, but worse, in Wonderland. A place where anything is possible and the consequences are great."

I shrugged. "I don't know. I guess I just care about him."

Malcolm frowned. "In what way?"

"As a friend kind of way. I care about the entire group of course. But you all seem to pick on him the most and team up on him. It doesn't seem fair when all he has been doing has been helping you guys travel to here from Wonderland."

He let out a sigh. "We only pick on him because he usually starts a fight. You don't know him like we do, Alice. Before the Nightmare Circus, he was rogue and causing a lot of problems, especially for our group. If it weren't for you, he wouldn't be part of this. He would still be some stray cat that causes chaos no matter where he went."

The argument was getting out of hand. It had been a while since Chase joined the group, so it made no sense why he was still holding on to so much anger. "I'm just saying to think what it is like in his shoes. You don't know what he's been through."

"And you think he tries to put himself in our shoes? Because he doesn't. He never has. He is selfish, Alice. I don't get why all the Alice's always side with him!"

I let go of Malcolm's hand and folded my arms. "Am I just a replacement for her? Is that how you see me?"

He shook his head as he tried to grab my shoulders. I stepped back and he sighed. "No, Alice, you are completely different."

"Were you and she a couple?"

He bit his lip. "Alice, that's complicated…"

I turned and ran off. I knew it was petty, but I didn't like how he was bringing her up. So what if the other Alice sided with Chase, did that mean I couldn't too? He had always been kind to me and wanted me to be safe. I couldn't turn my back on a friend like that.

Malcolm didn't chase after me like I thought he would. He must have known I just wanted to cool down, but it still ate at me. Didn't he care that I was angry with him? I felt like I was acting childish, but so were they.

Surprisingly, I didn't run into any of the others like I thought I would have. This place was bigger than I imagined, and I hoped I didn't do something stupid by running away from our group. I checked the time on my phone. I still had ten minutes before I had to meet up at the bus. I knew where the parking lot was from here, as I was getting better at directions.

I made my way to the fountain that lay in the middle of the gardens and sat on the edge of it, staring out at the rows of roses. It was quite lovely here, I had to admit. If only I didn't start a fight with Malcolm, then we would be enjoying it together. I sighed. I should just go back and tell him I was sorry for overreacting, but he needed to realize I was my own person and not the same Alice of legend. I didn't like to be compared to her. Not now, not ever.

As I started to stand, I noticed something in the reflection of the water in the fountain. I bent closer, trying to make out the figure. I turned my head to make sure no one was standing behind me. What was that illusion?

The figure in the water began to take shape, and I realized all too late that it was Morpheus. He was wearing his battered top hat and coat. I started to back away, but something reached for me from the water and pulled me toward it.

"Malcolm! Help!"

Those were the last words I was able to say before I plunged into the water.

And then I fell down... and down... and down.

Chapter 12

Was this actually happening, or was I dreaming again?

Everything was dark and I was falling down. I never had one of the dreams, or passing out, and causing me to feel like I was plunging into darkness. Traveling to Wonderland was the only reason for traveling down, so it meant only one thing.

Morpheus somehow opened a portal and was taking me to Wonderland.

How this was possible, I had no idea. Everyone said there was no sign of him being able to transport to this world, so he inevitably had help. If that were the case, then did it mean that the White Rabbit was helping Morpheus? Or was there something else going on?

As I fell, I realized that after all this time since the circus was destroyed, I never actually had come face-to-face with Morpheus. Would he be like he appeared in my dreams? Or was that just how he wanted me to see him?

My heart began to race. I would be utterly alone in this, and I didn't even know if the others would realize I was gone before it was too late. How much time would pass here before they saw I was gone? It might have been only half an hour for them, but it could be weeks for me. Would I survive? Would I defeat him or be able to get away and escape to the palace? Where would I even land?

As if the universe wanted to answer my questions, I stopped falling and hit the ground. The light was overcast with gray clouds above me. I felt the crunch of dead grass under my body and looked around to find I was correct—the area around me was all brown and appeared as if it hadn't been watered in quite some time. Dead hedges and bushes stretched out as far as I could see—almost appearing like a maze. On the hedges, I noticed flowers that still appeared red.

As if they had been painted that color.

"Oh my gosh… I'm in the Heart Kingdom," I whispered.

Morpheus clapped. I spun around to find him standing there, looking exactly as he did in my dreams. He had his tattered hat and coat and appeared as if he hadn't had a haircut in all the time he had been hiding. His beard was scraggly, and gray was speckled throughout.

He kept clapping. "Good guess, my dear Alice. It seems you know your stories."

"Why did you bring me here?" I asked as I stood and backed away from him.

He laughed. "I have already told you many times; I need you in order to enact my revenge on your world and Wonderland."

"You spoke of how it was unfair that the citizens of Wonderland died when dreams in my world fell apart. Why then do you want to destroy Wonderland? It makes no sense!"

"Because I want all the ties to your world completely destroyed and to make a new Wonderland where we are no longer entwined!"

"How do you know that is possible? How do you know if you destroy Wonderland now, if it will cut ties to my world? What if it just destroys both and then there is no Wonderland nor Earth?"

Morpheus shrugged. "Then it will be the end of everyone's pain and suffering. But first I need the key to it all…"

He started for me, and I spun on my heel and darted into the maze.

"Get back here! There is no escape from me this time!"

I didn't care what he said and kept on running. The hedges might have been dead, but that didn't mean there wasn't a maze I could try to lose him in. If I could find a way out of this maze before he caught up to me, I might be able to figure out which way the palace was and head straight there, if not find guards in another district to help me. No one was under Morpheus's spell any longer, at least that I knew of, and they all hated him, so it was possible for me to find someone to help.

Except first I had to find my way out of this maze. Since I was running, I couldn't try to logically think of how to make it to the exit. All I could do was run and hope for the best—which was not to turn in to a dead end. I really, really had to pray hard for that not to happen.

"Alice, you can't run from me!" I heard a voice call out. He sounded like he was coming from every direction. I didn't know what to do—for all I knew this could have been made by him and I was, in fact, dreaming. That would make the most sense, as he couldn't make portals to my world.

I shook my head. No, this was real. This was the Heart Kingdom, and I was trapped. I was alone. I had no one to come save me.

Even if the others traveled straight to Wonderland, they wouldn't be able to teleport here, not to mention if they even knew what had happened. I had run off from the others, and they might have no idea I was gone. It could be a while before I saw any sign of them.

Which meant I had to escape now before he caught up to me and imprisoned me.

The area smelled of dust and dried hay, like the fields on a late summer day. Sticks crunched under my shoes as I kept on running. I hoped he wasn't able to figure out where I was from the noise and that I was able to lose him. I glanced back to find him nowhere near. At least I had that going for me. Now I just needed to find a way out of here.

From what I could tell, there was no end in sight.

Kenny had mentioned it took him all day to paint the new buds of roses. Now it made sense—this area went on forever, or at least it felt like that. It could have just been because I was running for my life.

I was glad I was fit from dance being more intense at the advanced level as there was no way I could have run this much a couple of years ago. That, and I had been training for a while now in Wonderland. It was all for this.

I tripped a little but was able to catch myself. My heart was pounding in fear that I would trip yet again and embarrassingly get caught by Morpheus because of my clumsiness. Why I had to be like this, I did not know. It was just who I was, I supposed.

Turning a corner, I found that I was at a dead end. Crap. I quickly spun on my heels to turn the other way when I found Morpheus standing there, smiling. Without a second thought, I dove through the bush to try to get to the other side.

While it seemed logical at the time, I should have realized rosebushes had thorns. The points ripped at my clothes and caught in my skin. I held back my screams of pain as I forced myself to go farther into the hedge and out the other side. I didn't take a moment to stop to assess how bad I was bleeding but kept on moving forward.

"Get back here! You won't find an escape, I can guarantee that!" Morpheus called after me.

I didn't pay attention to his threat and kept on running. My skin burned where it had been cut, but I didn't care. Worse could be waiting for me if I let Morpheus catch up to me.

As I rounded a corner, I found Morpheus standing there. I turned around but not quick enough as he wrapped his arms around my torso.

"Ah, ah, ah! Don't struggle or you will leave me no choice but to drug you. Don't you want to find out what Wonderland poisons do to a human?"

I stopped struggling, acting as if I was going to cooperate, but the moment I felt his arms loosen, I kicked him in the leg.

"You brat!"

I tried to run forward, but he smacked his cane into my leg and I went straight down. I tried to gather myself but not before he stood above me and pulled the sword out of his cane.

"Resist any longer and I will make it so you can't. Do you understand?"

I glared at him. "Why not just kill me now? Then I can't stop you."

"Because I need you to draw the others here. And if you are hurt, they will more than likely kill me in a fit of rage. But I will hurt you if need be."

I slowly nodded as he helped me up, keeping his sword out just in case. I felt his threat wasn't empty, and I preferred to be in perfect health while trying to get away from this place or at least nothing worse than the thorn cuts. It was just him here from what I could tell. If I played my cards right, I would be able to escape eventually.

So I had to play it cool.

As I calmed down, he smiled. "Good, you are smarter than you look." He turned back around and led me toward the giant structure that was once the Heart Castle.

The castle itself was mostly in ruins, like that of the Black and White Kingdom, but you could tell it used to be grand. It looked like something out of Disney, although I guess Disney did make the Alice's *Adventures in Wonderland* movies. It looked more like Cinderella's castle though, with more red and black. It was mostly faded now, as time had longed passed since it was once a grand—and corrupt—kingdom. I wondered what it would have been like and how much of the cruelness in the stories were true.

Knowing Wonderland, it was probably worse than the stories, not to mention Chase and the others were commenting how the roses had to be red.

Part of the castle was still standing, and Morpheus led me to it. It was no wonder no one found him there. Not only was it huge but he could have easily hidden and maneuvered himself so no one could find him. Wonderland was also vast, and this was probably one part that they hadn't searched yet. Or he set up traps to notify him when people were around, then hid.

The last part of the castle that still had shape was one of the turrets. It appeared like something in a fairy tale —like Rapunzel—and stretched up high into the air. We didn't go up, however, but headed down into the lower level. Morpheus pulled me toward the staircase that seemed to go deeper and deeper into the ground. It had to be the dungeon, as dungeons always seemed to be on the lowest level. It made sense, I guessed, as then it was harder to escape. And most people hated basements. I personally found them to be spooky and fun. Other than this one though.

We got to the bottom level, and sure enough, it was full of dungeon cells. Morpheus threw me into one and locked the door. I was surprised the metal bars hadn't eroded after all this time. They appeared rather rusty, however, so I would have to make sure I didn't cut myself on it while trying to escape. Other than that, there were no windows or other way out. I was currently at his mercy.

"You have the key, right?" I asked as I folded my arms, uncomfortable with the situation. I didn't like the idea of being this deep in a castle with only one person around to be able to let me out. Who knew how long it would take the others to find me if something happened to Morpheus? I was screwed.

"Of course. I will need to take you out of here when they arrive so I can use you as a bargaining chip."

"And then what?" I asked.

He shrugged. "And then I will take over Wonderland. It's that simple."

That didn't seem simple. I sighed as I sat on the dusty cot. I had no idea how I was going to get out of this mess.

Chapter 13

What felt like a few hours passed and I had no idea if the sun was down or what time it was in Wonderland. Morpheus sat on a wooden stool, staring at me to make sure I did nothing to try to escape. I should have figured he would keep an eye on me, as he wasn't stupid. He didn't say anything, which I was glad for. I didn't need him trying to convince me that I sucked again. Right now I definitely felt helpless.

But he had to leave sometime. I just knew it.

I thought back on everything that had happened thus far. Morpheus somehow was able to enter my dreams and then was able to catch me off guard and drag me to Wonderland. Everyone else was either on Earth or searching for me right now. So what did the future hold? Was I going to escape, or was I going to have to wait for them to figure it out? I pondered that for hours, wondering what I should do next.

"What exactly do you see in Malcolm?" Morpheus asked. I jumped, surprised as he hadn't said two words to me the entire time.

I shrugged. "He's kind to me. Caring... A complete gentleman. He will do anything to keep me safe."

Morpheus gestured around. "Yet here you are."

"I mean... No one could have seen this coming. And it was more my fault anyway."

"Why were you alone in that garden? I thought I would have had to try harder to bring you to Wonderland without the others, but it was quite easy."

"I... We... It's none of your business." I folded my arms. I really didn't want to go into detail with him. He would just use it against me.

He smiled. "So you had a fight then. Oh, do tell."

I shook my head. "I already said it's none of your business."

Morpheus stood up and walked over to the cell. He leaned on the bars and stared at me with a smirk. "Let me take a guess... You asked him a question and he didn't answer."

I frowned. That was pretty accurate. I didn't know he could have known so much.

Oh right. He could read people's minds.

"I don't like you reading my mind. Please stop."

"I'm not reading your mind. That takes too much of

my power, and I need all that I have to defeat the Mad Hatter. No, I'm just making conclusions from what I know of you and of Malcolm."

"So he has always kept secrets?" I asked. I knew I shouldn't have pried into Malcolm's past, but after the little fight we had, I needed to know if I was the only one he did this to. I wasn't sure which scenario would be more reassuring, however. I didn't like the idea that he kept secrets from everyone, but I also didn't like if it was just me.

Morpheus laughed. "He is only secrets. Nothing he says is true. He only says what you want to hear to keep you around."

I shook my head. "No, that's not true. He has told me plenty."

"Has he told you your true role in Wonderland then?"

With everything going on, I had forgotten Morpheus had mentioned that in one of the dreams. And there was the fact that he didn't like the idea of me staying in Wonderland. Did it have to do with my role? Or was it something else?

"No. But he probably has a good reason, not to mention none of the others have told me either."

Morpheus laughed again. "Oh, Alice. You are way too trusting. You do not understand what this world is really like and go about playing little games with your so-called friends. They haven't been truthful to you—

they aren't giving you the information you need to know."

"And what information is that?"

"As I said—your role in Wonderland."

"It was to defeat you. Just like the other Alice, I come when there is trouble and I have to help fight with the power that is inside."

"No, silly Alice. There is much more than that. Alice has the role to completely change Wonderland if she wanted to. The last Alice left before she could do such a thing."

"But didn't she help take down the Heart Kingdom and then the Red and White Kingdom?"

He shrugged. "Even if she didn't come, they would have eventually taken down those kingdoms. No, the previous Alice knew of her true power, and that was why she left."

"If she held such power, why would she leave?" I asked, not quite buying into all that he was saying. Taking down kingdoms took a lot of power and theoretically changed Wonderland, even if it was what the people wanted.

"Because there would be many people trying to kidnap her and control her. If she was influenced by the wrong people, chaos could ensue."

"Like what you are doing now?"

He laughed. "You are catching on quickly. Although I moreso want you to draw out your little friends."

I wasn't sure what to think about being powerful enough to change anything I wanted about Wonderland. It didn't seem possible, and I felt that he was lying to me.

But then why had it felt like Malcolm was keeping something from me as well?

While I wasn't going to completely accuse Malcolm of hiding this from me, I was going to demand an answer of what was really going on once I got out of here and was in the clear. I have had a lot of fun in Wonderland, at least after we had defeated the circus. I would even consider this place home if given the chance. I cared about my friends here and have even grown close to Malcolm.

But we had never discussed the future.

I wondered if there was more to this and whether I would always be able to come to Wonderland. I glanced at Morpheus, who was still watching me.

"How long do I have before I have to leave this place?" I asked. I knew he would probably lie to me, seeing that it was a worry that I couldn't always come back.

"Once you are seventeen, you will no longer be able to come to Wonderland."

That was what I was afraid of, although I figured it eighteen, but I was wrong. I had a year left. Only a year. And then what?

"And there is too much here for Malcolm, or any of

the others, to stay with you. And given how important you are, and powerful, I doubt any of them would let you stay. As for telling you… if they haven't already, perhaps they never were going to. Perhaps they were just going to disappear one day and you would just have to forget about them."

I frowned but didn't answer. That was probably what Malcolm wanted to tell me, but something kept holding him back. I tried not to get angry at Malcolm, as I knew Morpheus was trying to twist things to make me turn against my friends. But there still were secrets the group wasn't sharing with me. Whether it was what Morpheus was telling me or if it was something else, I wasn't sure.

"What about you, Morpheus? What is your role? The others said you appeared out of nowhere but don't really have a role. What's your story?"

He let out a small laugh and went back to his chair. "My role? That is a long story."

"Well, it's not like I'm going anywhere."

"Fair enough. Well then, I will tell you, mostly because you won't have time to tell the others, although it wouldn't matter if you did. The cards already have been dealt for all of us in Wonderland."

I wasn't sure what he meant by that. Did he believe that fate was already determined in this world? Did he think everything he was doing was what he was supposed to be doing, no matter what the price was? I didn't ask as I waited for his story.

"I used to be a dream, just like the rest of the citizens of Wonderland. You have to realize, not all dreams actually know what they are. Mainly, the people with roles know about the dreams, and although the citizens know they are called dreams, they don't know what that actually means. Most have no clue they are tied to another world or that another world exists, yet we are at its mercy.

"One day I found out the truth—that I was tied to some human in your world and I grew angry and resentful. I did not want to die. I could feel my human connection begin to waver, as if they were giving up on their dream and thus killing me. So I thought to myself, what if someone else was having the same dream as the one that this person was having, and therefore more parts of me exist?

"Funny thing, Wonderland. Did you know there are many dreams that look identical? Quite a few. They are just spread out through different districts and typically don't run into each other. You probably never noticed because we are practically background characters to those who have roles."

I bit my lip. Now that he mentioned it, I didn't really know what many of the citizens were like as I had always worked with Malcolm and the others and didn't take real note. Maybe I had run into similar dreams and had never realized it.

"I was able to find all the dreams that were like me. Some were younger, some were older, but we were all the same. And somehow, by some miracle of magic, we were able to combine and become eternal, so to speak. You see, not every dream is unique in your world, even though many want to believe that it is. So therefore we can be eternal."

"But if that were the case, then why did you use the dark circus to destroy dreams? Why not just search for matching dreams and do the same to them as you did to yourself?"

He nodded, as if agreeing. "Yeah, I tried that, but it didn't work for some reason. That was why I came up with the idea of destroying all the dreams currently and then starting over—finding a way to disconnect from your world and giving them what they deserve."

I really couldn't argue with that. He had good reasoning. Immoral, yes, but he really did want Wonderland to change.

"So you want to play God and destroy the world to make it new. Like the great flood or something similar."

"I'm not sure what you are talking about, but sure. I'll play God or the villain or whatever to free Wonderland of the connection."

"But how do you know that's what the rest of Wonderland wants? How do you know it's not something they just accepted already?"

"Because they—"

A bell chimed and Morpheus turned. I wondered if it was the others and they already figured out where I was. That didn't seem possible, however, as they hadn't seen me get captured.

"I will be right back. It seems I have a guest."

He left the room, and I took a deep breath. This was my chance to escape.

Although my hair was short, I had started using bobby pins to keep my hair back. This was due to doing more moves in dance and my bangs always hitting straight in my eyes and because Chase taught me to learn how to pick a lock with them, so I never was without one. With Morpheus on the loose, I always kept some bobby pins at the ready.

Apparently all the bobby pins I had worn, and lost, were worth it.

I unbent one bobby pin to be a lockpick and bent the other to be my tension wrench. Now I just needed to keep enough pressure and hold that tension while I worked at each pin and tried to push them each in enough until it clicked. I practiced a lot in my world, which was actually one reason I'd gotten detention with Chase. He wanted me to practice under pressure. Let's just say I wasn't fast enough.

Once I felt them all click, I watched as the lock turned, and I was able to push open the cell door.

Now I just had to figure out how to get out of here

without him finding me. But first thing was first. I quickly went over and grabbed a sword and Morpheus's canteen of water. I shook it to find it mostly full. Who knew how long it would be before I would find someone to help me? I didn't see any food, but at least I had some Kind granola bars in my jacket pocket.

I recalled how to get through the corridors and which staircases to use. I kept an ear out for Morpheus, but I didn't hear him anywhere. As I made my way up the staircase, I found the coast was clear.

Not sure which way to go, I chose one direction and ran toward the forest.

Chapter 14

I ran and ran until my legs could not go any farther. I stopped and turned to see if Morpheus had figured out what happened and followed. He would have had to discern which way I had headed, which was nearly impossible as there were many routes to take from the castle. But just in case, I hadn't slowed down for what felt like an hour. As I looked back, I didn't see anything in these dense woods except for fog and flowers and…

Now that I wasn't running for my life, I realized where I had entered. This was the Dark Forest.

"Crap," I whispered as I scanned around. Pansies surrounded me, and I quickly covered my ears as they started to sing. I had to keep moving unless I wanted to pass out and never be found again. I couldn't go back, as Morpheus would be looking for me, so there was only one way to go—forward.

Although I was starting to get used to hearing the song of these flowers, that didn't mean I was going to let my guard down. Chase and I came back here a couple of times so I could get used to the sound, but last time I passed out because I thought I was used to it. Malcolm never knew we did that as he would have forbidden me from coming here.

Well, it looks like it was a good idea because now I found myself trapped here.

I was able to make it through the field of flowers, and I stopped to really take in where I was. I took a deep breath, trying to calm myself down. Okay, so I was stuck in the Dark Forest by myself. I hadn't been any deeper than the flowers since we came here to run away from Morpheus. That was months ago in my world. I'd barely made it out alive with friends helping.

I had a choice: turn around and hope I could reach the edge, or go around the forest and pray Morpheus didn't think I would be stupid enough to run in here and would be looking for me on the other side of the castle.

So I would just backtrack and go around. Yeah, that was the best choice. I should have done it right when I figured out where I was, but fear was still clouding my judgment.

Turning around, I started back toward the singing

flowers that lined the entire forest. It shouldn't be too far since I had just walked straight from them. I made sure not to turn or anything while I was walking so that I wouldn't get too lost.

The trees were as eerie as always with moss hanging off them and their branches appearing scraggly. A thick mist covered the ground, and I prayed the soft ground I stepped on was because of moss and not something else. I just prayed nothing would suddenly grab me and pull me under like in *Star Wars*. Or that I wasn't, in fact, inside a worm.

That didn't seem likely, but something grabbing me did, as I had been attacked by a giant spider earlier. I was glad I snagged a sword before I left the prison and held it tightly in my hands. I would not drop it if I got spooked—I wouldn't.

I kept on walking back toward where I believed the flowers were and the edge of the forest. After half an hour, I didn't come across them.

"Crap on a cracker."

I was lost. Already. I didn't understand how I could have gotten turned around within a few minutes. I knew I was clumsy, but this was on a whole different level.

I was screwed.

The smartest thing to do was to go in a straight line and pray that I ended up picking a short distance to anywhere out of here. If I kept changing direction, then there was the chance that I would never be able to find a way out.

I was really glad I grabbed water as I left. I guess I did learn a thing or two about surviving from Malcolm and Chase. This definitely wasn't anything I learned from school. I took a small sip of the water and prayed the canteen would last until I got out of the forest.

There was a chance Malcolm would be able to find me in this forest, as he knew this area like the back of his hand, or so he said. But first he would have had to realize I was missing, find Morpheus, figure out I had run away, and then come to the conclusion I was stupid enough to run into the forest.

No, I would have to find a way out myself or I might be stuck in the Dark Forest for days.

I kept forward, ignoring the rustling in the bushes and the sound of the Jabberwocky roaring in the distance. I kept telling myself that I had a sword and that I would be fine. I would probably be out of here before the end of the day, as the odds were I wasn't going through the center of the forest. No, it was more likely that I would find a shorter path.

If luck were on my side at least. Let's be honest—so far, it hadn't been.

Flashbacks to the last time I was in this forest entered my mind. What all did I need to worry about? There were those giant spiders, the Jabberwocky, the weird blue lights, the trisings, the flowers... Yeah, that's all I remembered so far. I tried to recall if there were any other things that we had fought. I knew that once the sun set, there were many creatures in these parts that I didn't want to deal with. I would have to find somewhere to sleep. Malcolm had found us a cave each night, as he knew where they were all located. I had no idea and just prayed I would come across something.

Trekking forward, I hoped that I would find a way out quickly. I did not want to try to spend a night in this forest. How would I catch a trising? I didn't even have a jar, not to mention I didn't think I could actually catch one on my own. Then there still was the fact I hadn't spotted any caves yet.

There was no way I would survive through a night here. I was not that crafty and there were too many things wanting to eat me. I made a mental note, however, to ask Malcolm to train me to be able to fight those monsters in case I found myself in here again on my own. Then I would have one less thing to fear.

I picked up my speed, not wanting to slow down for anything. If I walked faster, I could get out of here faster, right? It made sense to me. I just tried to be careful where I stepped, not wanting to fall and get dragged away by the giant spider. Again.

Coming up to an opening, I prayed it was a way out. It wasn't, unfortunately, but it was a part of the Dark Forest I remembered coming across last time. A table lay in the middle of the area, covered in moss and fallen leaves. It was the Mad Hatter Tea Party.

I stopped, promising myself I would remember which way I had been heading. I had to look over this place again as I wanted to learn more. Last time I was here, Malcolm had said he didn't know what this was. The others hadn't said anything, but I'd known he was lying.

He didn't want me to know about his time in the Dark Forest.

There was a lot about Wonderland that I didn't understand, including its past. There was a lot of darkness surrounding Wonderland, and Malcolm was in the middle of it all. I couldn't find all my answers here, but I knew I could uncover some truth.

I started ripping away the moss, the soft, moist feeling tickling my hands. Bugs ran as they had been unearthed for the first time in forever. I uncovered teacups, as I expected, and saucers of all different sizes and designs. Nothing seemed out of the ordinary.

Until I started to pull out bones.

I dropped one and it crashed on the ground, breaking into a few pieces. What the heck? Why were there bones?

There were other bones. I couldn't tell if they were human or animal, as I wasn't the best at biology, but it was still strange to find so many. As I searched more, I found a skull. Worms crawled all through the eyes, like something out of a horror movie. It was a skull that couldn't have been anything other than human.

I started breathing rapidly. What was this? What could have happened here?

Chase always commented on how dark Malcolm was. Could he have killed these people? And if he had, was it out of self-defense, or was there something else that had happened in the woods? I couldn't imagine Malcolm hurting anyone unless he had to, like Morpheus or something. Even then I couldn't imagine him killing someone—just overpowering them and arresting them. But for him to kill in cold blood... He couldn't be that dark.

I turned back toward the way I was heading and picked up my pace. I had to get away from there and forget what I had seen. Davis and Melvin were also with Malcolm in the Dark Forest, and they wouldn't have stayed with him if he was such a monster. I needed to stop believing Morpheus and letting him give me doubts about Malcolm. I needed to trust him. There was more to the story than met the eye.

I heard the scream of a Jabberwocky in the distance behind me, which led me to believe I was going in the right direction—away from the monsters.

The trees were getting denser, and I had to push the vines and hanging moss out of my way. Did this mean I was traveling toward the exit or not? Doubt filled my mind, and I didn't know if I was walking in the right direction. But I couldn't change my way or I might never be able to get out of here. So I needed to stick with the way I was going and hope for the best.

A howling from the left made me jump. It sounded like wolves, but I didn't remember any type of wolf being in these woods. Perhaps it was something kind and cuddly. I knew that wasn't the case, but I had to keep telling myself that so my legs would move forward.

I used the sword to cut away some of the vines and prayed that they wouldn't become alive and grab me or that one of them was a snake. Sweat dripped off my face, and I took several sips of water. I would definitely need a Gatorade after this, as I felt as if my electrolytes were depleting and I was getting dehydrated.

A couple of hours had passed, and I noticed the sun was starting to go down and it was getting darker. Crap. Crap. Crap. I needed to get out of here. My adrenaline was slowing down, and I felt tired and weak. I just wanted to find a bed and sleep forever.

And that was when I saw it—the field of flowers that indicated I was on the edge of the forest. Whether I was heading toward the Heart Castle or if I made it out the other side, there was only one way to find out.

I plugged my ears and ran as fast as I could.

Chapter 15

The sun was setting as I stepped out of the very edge of the Dark Forest. I didn't see the Heart Castle anywhere within sight, which was a good thing. At least now I didn't have to worry about Morpheus finding me. All I had to do was find someone to take me to the Dream Palace.

Unfortunately, wherever I was, I didn't see any buildings within sight. I sighed. Just my luck, although it made sense no one would want to live this close to the Dark Forest. Who knew what monsters could potentially escape?

Luckily I had my cell phone and could use it as a light if I needed, but the moon was out, and since this place didn't have pollution like Earth did, I could see better here in the dark than in the day in the Dark

Forest. I kept walking through the field, beautiful flowers blooming as far as the eyes could see. I was definitely in the District of Flowers. This place must have been larger than I remembered because I didn't recall a field this large and I didn't see the city anywhere.

But this was better than the Dark Forest.

I saw a dim light in the distance and wanted to cry in relief. I was almost there. I would finally find someone to take me to the Dream Palace.

As I got closer, I found a little girl about eleven or so in the yard, playing with flowers. As I approached, she ran inside and soon her father stepped outside.

"What is someone doing way out here?" he asked. From what I could tell, he was tall, muscular, and he had a thick beard. The light was still dark so I couldn't make out many other features.

"I am on the run from Morpheus and need to get to the Dream Palace as soon as possible. If you have some form of transportation, can I borrow it or can you take me?" My stomach growled. "And maybe a light snack."

The man gestured to the door. "Please come inside. We were just about to have dinner and have plenty to go around."

I nodded. "Thank you so much."

As I stepped inside, the mother, a woman with dark brown hair and a simple floral dress, gasped. "Oh dear, you look awful! What happened to you?"

I glanced down to find my clothes ripped and dried blood crusted all over my body. "Uh, yeah. I was in the Dark Forest."

The couple stared at me. "The Dark Forest? And you survived?"

I nodded. "I'm here, so I guess? Let me explain. I am Alice, and I was kidnapped by Morpheus who wants to take over Wonderland. I must get to the king and queen and let them know what happened."

They glanced at each other, and the lady nodded. "You are welcome to stay the night here. It would be better to travel in the day, and you need to rest."

I shook my head. "No, I need to get there now. I don't want them to worry any longer, and I don't want to put your family in danger if Morpheus figures out where I went. The safest thing to do is to take me now… or after some food if that is okay."

The man let out a breath. "Fine. I can take you after we eat. But first let's get you a change of clothes and washed up. I don't want people to have the wrong idea as we travel."

He had a point, so I nodded. "That sounds like a deal. What are your names?"

"Zachariah and Penny Klein. And our daughter's name is Katherine," Zachariah said.

Penny took my hand. "Come, I should have something that will fit you. Then I can show you where to wash up, and then we can eat."

"I'm so sorry to intrude like this."

She shook her head. "It is the least we can do for the kingdom."

I followed her up the stairs and into her bedroom. It was quaint but relaxing as I felt this family really loved each other. I prayed that Morpheus didn't find out where I was for fear that something would happen to this family. I wouldn't be able to live with myself if that were the case.

Penny pulled out a beige-and-pink floral dress and set it on the bed. They must really like flowers as that was what they farmed and because of the district they lived in. She filled up the tub a little so I could use the water to wash my skin.

"I will be downstairs if you need anything. Food will be waiting."

"Thank you very much. I appreciate it."

She closed the door and I took my clothes off, grimacing as the fabric stuck to the cuts from the rosebushes. I grabbed a rag and cleaned the cuts gently and washed away all of the excess blood. Once I was cleaned off, I wouldn't bleed on the dress Penny had given me.

I put it on. It actually fit me perfectly, and I liked the style. Maybe I would find more dresses like this in my world, as they seemed to be the new trend lately. I grabbed my clothes and headed down the stairs. I placed my soiled clothes near the door where my shoes were and went to the dining table where the family had been waiting. Some bread and a large pot filled with meat, carrots, onions, and potatoes sat on the table. It looked amazing, and my stomach rumbled again.

"Thank you so much." I sat down at the free spot across from Katherine. She smiled at me, a little shy.

"It is no problem," Zachariah said. He served each of us, and I almost drooled. I waited for him to finish serving everyone and to take the first bite. He didn't say grace or anything like that, which I guess made sense since Christianity didn't exist here. It was why I waited, however, as I had awkwardly eaten before Kate's family said grace before. I learned my lesson the first time.

The food was delicious, and I tried not to appear like a pig as I ate, but I did finish before everyone else. It almost looked as if I had licked my plate clean.

"Would you like seconds?" Penny asked.

I shook my head. "No, I am fine. Thank you so much for the meal—it has been a while since I have eaten anything this tasty."

"Your words are too kind." Penny blushed.

"I will return this dress as soon as I am able. At the palace, I have a change of clothes…"

She shook her head. "No, feel free to keep it. I have more like it, and it suits you very well. Call it a gift for saving Wonderland. If it weren't for you, our daughter wouldn't be alive."

I wasn't sure what she meant by that, but I nodded. "You are most welcome."

The others finished their food while I waited patiently. I was glad to be out of the Dark Forest and away from Morpheus, but I wasn't in the clear yet. There was still the matter of getting to the palace and finding Malcolm and the others. Then I would be able to relax. I didn't like being here longer than I needed and risking their lives.

Zachariah wiped his face clean and stood up. "Well, shall we head to the palace? It is about an hour out, but I will need to set up the wagon and horse."

I nodded. "Yes, let me know what I can do to help."

"I could use a hand with the dishes. If that is all right."

I nodded and assisted Penny in gathering the dishes and put them in the sink. She washed them off while I dried.

"You know," she began as she handed me a plate. "Nothing really remarkable ever happened here until the circus came. We mostly stay out here on the farm unless we need to go into town for supplies. There are some other farms around and families we know, but it was always the same ol' thing for a while. So when the circus came, we just had to see it for ourselves."

I kept quiet as she told her story.

"Never did I imagine that it would almost destroy our family and life. There was so much fear and darkness surrounding that place. I should have gotten Zachariah to turn around. But Katherine wanted to see the circus, so we stayed. Then we were encased in fear. Katherine became very sick, and we couldn't do anything to stop it. Everyone had been affected by that point. It wasn't until you lifted the curse that our family was saved."

I blushed. Although I knew what I did helped restore Wonderland, hearing such a personal story like that was different. "It was only partially me, honest. The real heroes are Malcolm and the rest of the guardians. They brought me here and taught me everything I needed to know."

"You mean a lot to the people though, just remember that. The others play their parts, but you are something else entirely."

I nodded as I dried off another plate. "Thank you."

Zachariah came back in and smiled. "Are you ready?"

"Yes." I turned to Penny and Katherine. "Thank you so much for the meal. I am very grateful."

"You are most welcome. Feel free to come visit anytime."

Zachariah led me out to where the wagon was. It was similar to the one in *Spice and Wolf*—simple with room to keep supplies and whatever they would be selling. I got in next to Zachariah, a little excited to experience this. Usually we traveled with Chase, which was very convenient I now realized. But this would be an adventure in and of itself.

He made a clicking noise with his tongue and moved the reins. The horse started off at a good pace. I glanced around, barely making anything out with the moonlight. Although I could distinguish some flowers, I knew that much of what was hidden from me was beautiful. I would have to come back to see it again.

Zachariah and I didn't say much as we headed toward the palace area. I admired the full moon, wishing I could stare at up the stars with Malcolm. Once this was over, we would be free of having to deal with Morpheus, and we could enjoy the small things. That is, if I got to stay in Wonderland once Morpheus was caught. What if they just kicked me out? What if the only reason they kept me around was to find Morpheus?

I bit my lip. Was Malcolm just nice because he wanted me to stay? No, that couldn't be the only reason. He cared—I knew that had to be a fact. I just needed to figure out the entire truth and why he kept me around. That was all.

"So once you get to the palace, will you be able to stop Morpheus once and for all?" Zachariah asked.

I nodded. "I hope so. If not, then I don't know what we will do to catch him."

"A lot of the citizens are afraid of him, especially after what he did. He might have disappeared, but that doesn't mean we have felt safe. Once you imprison him, the people will be much happier, I can guarantee that."

"Many were affected. Your wife said that even your daughter was caught under that dark spell."

"Yes. It was terrifying. We couldn't do anything and our own fear grew. We didn't know if we would survive. Some of our neighbors didn't. Many citizens vanished. But luckily you came and stopped it before all of Wonderland was destroyed."

"With the help of others, yes. I am glad they were there to lead me and were able to find me. I just hope this will be the last of Morpheus."

"As do I."

We rode for an hour, just as Zachariah said, and found ourselves at the edge of the inner kingdom. I could see the wondrous palace in the distance as it stretched up high in the sky. I loved that it felt dreamy here, as it was the Dream Kingdom, and there were floating lights and soft colors. It was one of my favorite places in all of Wonderland.

Leading us toward the palace, Zachariah took the trade route into town. Most of the pathways in the kingdom were for pedestrians, but some roads were designated for travelers and traders only. There weren't many people out as it was late in the night for the road, but I could see people walking the streets and crowding the markets. It almost appeared as if that part of the city never slept.

As we came up to the palace, Zachariah dropped me off.

"Thank you again for taking me all the way out here. If there is anything you need, just let me know and I will try my best to get it granted."

He shook his head. "No, you have done enough for me and my family already. It is the least I can do. I better hurry back before it is too late. Take care of yourself."

With that, he left me there. I turned and entered the palace grounds. Two guards recognized me and came up to me.

"Alice! What are you doing in the Kingdom of Dreams? Where are the others?"

"I have information on Morpheus and need to speak to the king and queen right away!"

Chapter 16

The guard brought me to the king and queen, who were playing live chess with the White Rabbit watching. No one was actually getting killed though, but it was strange to see people playing the pieces. I was surprised they still played such a game, even after the Red and White Kingdom was destroyed, as they were tied to chess pieces. I guess some things just never changed.

The game stopped the moment I walked in. The queen hurried over to me. "Alice! What are you doing here? Where are the others?"

"Morpheus kidnapped me, but I was able to escape. I'm not sure if the others even realize I am gone."

"Morpheus?" the king exclaimed. "You found him?"

"Well, he found me, but yes. We need to get in touch

with Malcolm and Kenny and—"

A voice shouted from the corridor. "We need to see the king and queen at once! Alice has been captured! She—" Malcolm walked in and saw me standing there. He ran up to me and wrapped his arms around me. "Alice! Great kingdoms, how did you end up here?"

Chase and the others walked in and saw me as well.

"Alice!" Davis squeaked as they all ran to me. I was never so glad to see someone before.

"Now, Alice, how about we all sit down and you tell us the entire story." The queen ushered the chess pieces away. They all left, and we moved to the lounge area. Malcolm took a seat next to me on the chair, and the rest gathered around.

"When we were in the Rose Garden, I ran off toward a fountain. While I was sitting there, something grabbed me and pulled me into this world. I found myself in the middle of the Heart Kingdom. Morpheus was waiting for me, and I tried to run, but he caught me in the maze. Then he threw me in a cell, but someone appeared in the Heart Kingdom, and he left to see who it was. I was then able to use my hairpin to pick the lock, and I ran. Unfortunately I ran straight into the Dark Forest."

Davis's eyes widened. "You went into the Dark Forest alone?"

I nodded as I glanced over at Malcolm. I would need to talk to him later but knew this was not the time. He seemed as nervous as the rest of them though, and that made me feel a little better.

"Yeah. I was able to find my way out before it became dark and wandered to the Flower District. Luckily I found a farmer who was willing to bring me here."

Malcolm grabbed my hand. "I am glad you are safe. I was so worried. We had no idea what happened."

"How did you figure out I was kidnapped?" I asked.

Malcolm nodded toward Chase. "He saw you get taken. He was up in a tree. He tried to get to you before you disappeared but he wasn't fast enough. He quickly found us and we came straight here."

So they did know right away. Morpheus was right. And only minutes passed for them when it was hours here. That was terrifying to think about.

I explained what Morpheus said. "Morpheus used to be a dream. He realized what he was and didn't want to die, so he found everyone who was the same dream as him and somehow used magic to combine each other. He doesn't want anyone else to die like he almost did; he wants to destroy this world and start anew. To do that, he thinks he needs to destroy all of you first."

Bill laughed. "He thinks he can go up against all of us? He is mad."

I shrugged. "If it's just him. I mean, someone did come to the castle. If it wasn't all of you, who could it have been other than an insider?"

Everyone was silent. I knew I had a point.

"It could have been a bird," Chase said. "Like when our alarm would go off in the Black and White Kingdom."

"That's true," I said. "But it could have also been whoever was keeping him hidden."

"We checked the Heart Kingdom," the White Rabbit said. "There was no sign of anyone living there."

"Which means he was moving around," Malcolm explained. "And that he does have someone helping him move around. Alice is right. There is no way he could be doing this by himself."

"But who could be helping?" Chase asked. "And why?"

Melvin spoke up. "There is probably something else going on behind the scenes. Whoever is helping Morpheus could be using him as a pawn and doesn't actually want his Wonderland but us out of the way so they can make their own Wonderland. If we are gone, that leaves Alice on her own, and they will try to use her."

"If that is the case"—Malcolm sighed—"we need to figure out who it is. We need answers."

"The best way to figure out who is behind this is to bring Morpheus in for questioning. We shall go to the Heart Kingdom in the morning and attack," Bill said as he turned to the king and queen. "As long as you decree it."

The queen nodded. "Yes, of course. Anything to keep our dear Alice safe. Just tell us what you need, and we will provide it."

The king nodded in agreement, and I turned to Malcolm and whispered, "What should I do?"

"You will need to come to show us where he was keeping you. The Heart Kingdom is large, and without you being able to point out where to go, we won't be able to sweep it fast enough. And then you will be free of your nightmares." He smiled.

I returned his smile, glad that I could be a part of the attack but also that I would no longer have to worry about Morpheus entering my dreams. However, now we believed that there was someone else involved, possibly pulling the strings. If that were the case, would they keep trying to come after me? Would Morpheus reveal who it was? How long would that take, and once we figured out who it was, would I have to leave Wonderland for good?

The truth was I didn't want to leave this place. I wanted to be able to travel forever. This place was everything I could ever dream of, even if some parts were scary. Most were so kind, and I felt as if I could belong. But what if I couldn't go back to my world? There was a lot for me there as well, and I couldn't just disappear, or my family would be devastated. So what would I do if I was given a choice? Would I even be given a choice?

No, I would wait until all this was over to get my answers and figure out my future. First thing was first —we had to capture Morpheus.

"You all should get some rest, especially Alice as she has had such an ordeal," the queen proclaimed.

"We will discuss everything in the morning," the White Rabbit explained as he wound his pocket watch. "And none of you better be late."

"But what if he leaves before then?" I asked. "Shouldn't we go there right now?"

Malcolm placed his hand on my back. "You said Morpheus wanted us to come to him and that was why he kidnapped you. Since you escaped, he knows you will lead us straight to him, so he still gets his wish. I think he will be waiting for us. We will have to be extra careful, however, as he will set traps and the like. Giving Bill the entire night will also help him prepare the men and find the old maps of the Heart Kingdom. Meanwhile, you can rest."

That made sense, I supposed. I was pretty tired after everything and needed a good night's rest. I doubted Morpheus would enter my dreams since he needed all his powers for the battle that was to come.

"Now go get some sleep. I will stop by later to make sure you are fine, okay?" Malcolm kissed the top of my head.

I blushed and nodded. I left the military unit to

figure out the rest while I headed to my room. As I walked into the hallway, I found the Duchess. She wore a similar elaborate dress as last time I had seen her, except this one was pink.

She ran over to me and wrapped her arms around me. It was strange, as I hardly knew her. "Oh, Alice! I am so glad you are all right. I had heard you had been kidnapped, and I just feared the worse!"

This felt like déjà vu. "I am fine now. Thanks?"

She backed away and peered into my eyes with her blue doll-like eyes. "I don't know what we would do without our wonderful Alice. Morpheus would be unstoppable if he had you in his clutches."

Again, someone inferring I was the key to Wonderland. I let out a breath. "Well I am fine now, so you have nothing to worry about."

Chase walked up to the two of us. "Evening, Duchess."

"Oh, my dear kitty cat. How have you been? Is everyone treating you like they should?" The Duchess patted his purple hair. Chase's cheeks turned red.

"I'm fine. I don't need you worrying about me."

"But I must. You were once my kitty after all."

Chase rolled his eyes, but the Duchess just smiled.

"Well, I better leave you two to get ready to attack Morpheus. I believe Wonderland can be peaceful once he is gone."

Chase grabbed my hand. "We better get going,

Duchess. I will see you later."

Pulling me off in the opposite direction, Chase seemed irritated. Once the Duchess was no longer visible, I pulled my hand away from Chase.

"What was that about?" I asked.

He shook his head. "She's bad news. I don't trust her."

"Didn't you used to work for her?"

"Who told you that?"

"Malcolm."

Chase shook his head. "He doesn't know the whole story. Or understand, for that matter."

"Then tell me your side."

"It's not the time or place. We need to focus on the attack right now. Some other time maybe."

"Okay."

Chase looked me over. "Don't worry, it's not because I don't trust you, it's just a lot of baggage that I don't want to unload on you when you need to get some rest. Oh, and by the way, that dress looks adorable on you."

I blushed. "Oh thanks. It was a farmer's wife's dress. She was very pretty and had a whole wardrobe of similar outfits."

"Well, I think this one looks perfect on you. I definitely think it is a look you can pull off. It sort of fits your artistic side."

"Yeah, I was going to find some dresses similar to it

at the mall when we get back. I think I saw some at JCPenney."

He smiled. "Can't wait. Now, come on. I will walk you to your room."

Chase and I headed down the hallway toward where my room was. I turned to him. "So why aren't you back planning with the others?"

He shrugged. "I don't really need to be. I'm just the one who opens the portals for these things. I don't come up with the plan and just check in at the end to make sure everything is fine and be told what I need to do."

"I guess that makes sense."

"I like it anyway, then no one can blame me for making up a bad plan. Instead, they will just blame me when I try to take things into my own hands."

He was referring to when Bill captured me during the attack on the Red and White Kingdom. That seemed so long ago, as months had passed since then. Now Bill was like a friend and we all worked together.

"That wasn't your fault. You were trying to do what you thought was best."

"Whatever, it was in the past. It all turned out fine in the end. And now we will finally finish it."

Which was strange to think about. After all this time, would my journey here be at an end? We had to find out who was really calling the shots, but what then?

"Chase… who do you think could be behind this?"

He frowned and shook his head. "I honestly don't know. It could be anyone."

"But wouldn't it have to be someone with roles? It couldn't be another dream, or at least I don't think it could be."

"I guess. But that is scary, is it not? I mean, there aren't many of us and most are our close friends."

He had a point. Was it someone on the inside? Was it someone in our group? There were so many unanswered questions that I didn't quite know if I wanted to find out the truth.

Because if it was someone on the inside, they had been lying to everyone all along.

We came upon my room, and I hesitated to go in, realizing that I didn't want to be alone right now. After everything that happened, I still feared that Morpheus could somehow capture me while in the palace.

Chase studied me for a moment. "Do you want me to stay? I understand if you do. Malcolm will probably come around soon anyway, and I can just keep you company until then."

I nodded. "Yeah, actually I would like that. I'm a little scared still."

Opening the door, we entered my room.

Chapter 17

Chase turned as I changed into my pajamas, which was a long gown like those in the old Victorian movies. It was strange sleeping in a dress, but it actually felt soft around my skin. I was already used to Chase and Malcolm seeing me in my pajamas, so I didn't mind. It wasn't like it was actually any different from regular clothes. Neither was a towel, yet everyone acted like it was revealing. No, a bikini was revealing, but no one cares about that. It was all so strange.

"Thank you again for staying here with me. Once I realized I would be alone, I started to panic."

Chase shook his head. "Not a problem. I mean, Malcolm is going to scold me, but I'll live."

"I think in this case, he will understand. As long as you don't transport me on the roof or something and we not tell them."

"That happened one time, and they will never stop bringing it up."

I laughed as I sat down on my bed. Although I was tired, I felt like I could talk with Chase for hours like this. I never realized how close we were until now. He and I could practically talk about anything, and it felt natural. It was almost like how I felt with Kate.

"Hey, Chase, can I ask you a question?" I knew this wasn't a good time, but I wasn't going to be able to sleep if I didn't at least ask one person about what Morpheus had said.

He sat on the bed next to me. "What is it?"

"Morpheus had said that I was the key to Wonderland and that I could shape Wonderland into whatever I wanted. What did he mean by that?"

Chase hesitated. "That's... complicated. You are special, Alice, and were able to stop Morpheus's circus."

I knew that wasn't what Morpheus meant. I sighed. "If you don't want to get in trouble by telling me, that's fine. I understand."

"Our world is complicated, Alice. I don't want you to get mixed up with some of the things that go on."

"But I am already mixed up with you all! I like helping everyone and being here! I don't want to leave! I don't want—" I stopped as my eyes started to fill will tears. "Sorry. It's been a long day. I think I will go to sleep."

Chase nodded, and I got under the covers. He went over and turned the light off.

"Good night, Alice. I will be here if you need me or at least until Malcolm gets here."

"Thank you. Good night."

It was a whisper, but I was able to barely hear it. "And I don't want you to leave either."

I awoke when I heard whispers.

"What are you doing here, cat?" It was Malcolm.

"I was watching over her to make sure Morpheus didn't try anything."

"I didn't give you permission to do such a thing."

I leaned up and rubbed my eyes to find Malcolm and Chase arguing. The little light from the hallway made it so I could identify them.

"I asked him to, Malcolm. I didn't want to be alone."

Malcolm walked over and sat at the edge of my bed. "I'm sorry I woke you. And fine, I guess I can let it slide since you requested it. I'm just used to this cat doing whatever he wants."

"Whatever," Chase commented as he stepped out of the room. "Good night, Alice."

"Good night, Chase," I said as he left Malcolm and I.

"So, do you guys have a plan of action?"

"Yup. We are ready to go. Kenny is giving the details

to all the soldiers, and we will be set once morning comes."

"That's good."

He stroked my cheek. "You should get more rest. Everything will be ready in the morning."

Although I did want to go back to sleep, I also didn't want to sleep away the alone time with Malcolm before this battle. What if something happened tomorrow? Fear swept through my mind. What if Malcolm or anyone else got seriously hurt or worse?

"Hey, Malcolm?"

"What is it?"

"What if something happens tomorrow? What if someone…?"

"Shh, don't worry about it. There's no way Morpheus will be able to outdo us, and we have a lot of numbers compared to him. You have nothing to worry about."

"I was just so scared when I was captured. I didn't know if you had found out I was captured or how long it would take for you to get to Wonderland."

"Luckily it was quite fast, even though it was hours for you. I feel bad I couldn't have come sooner, but when I found out, I was so worried. I had feared the worst."

"I'm fine, thankfully."

"You are lucky. I'm glad the tricks we taught you got you out of the cell, but you could have died in the Dark

Forest."

"But I didn't."

He lay down next to me and leaned on his elbow as he caressed my hand. "Which is a miracle. You were able to find a short path out, which is not something many are able to do."

"I started walking straight and hoped for the best."

"You could have gone straight through the middle, which would have taken days."

"I know. I am really happy it ended the way it did. I had no way to survive the night." I bit my lip. "But I did come across something."

Malcolm's hand stopped moving for a second. "What was it?"

"The table... I found a table with teapots and other stuff."

"There are a lot of random things in the Dark Forest."

"But the stories..."

Malcolm placed his finger on my lips. "Don't worry about it. That is ancient history. What matters now is defeating Morpheus."

I noticed how he changed the subject. I felt that there was a lot going on that I didn't understand and stuff that happened so long ago that I couldn't begin to comprehend. But that didn't mean I didn't deserve an answer. I also deserved being told what was to happen after all this was over.

"I guess you are right. I should get some more rest."

"I will be here when you wake up."

I turned over and felt safe knowing he was next to me, but I still worried about the future. How would I ask him what's next after this was over? What if he didn't want me to stay? And why wouldn't he if he cared about me?

When I woke, Malcolm was lying next to me, asleep. I smiled, as he was adorable when he was sleeping. He must have been exhausted after going on the field trip and then finding out I was taken and then having to plan an attack. I know I was tired last night as well.

Malcolm stirred and his eyes flickered open. He smiled when he saw me.

"Good morning, beautiful. Ready to bring peace to Wonderland?"

I nodded. "Of course."

I got up and quickly changed into the men's-style clothing here. I felt it was the easiest for me to fight in rather than a dress. I wore a simple blue button-up shirt and beige pants with suspenders.

Coming back into the main bedroom area, I found Malcolm straightening his bow tie. "All set?"

"Yup. Let's find the others and head over to where Bill will be going over the plan of attack."

As I opened the door, I found Chase had been

leaning his back on it. He stumbled back and stared up from the ground.

"Hi, Alice."

"Good morning, Chase. Were you waiting long?"

He gathered himself up and grinned. "No, I just was waiting for you two so we could head to Bill's. The others are already there."

"You could have knocked, you know."

He shrugged. "It sounded like you two were about to come outside."

Malcolm sighed. "Then why were you leaning on the door?"

"Uh… Fine. I had been waiting for a while and dozed off."

Now that I looked at him, I realized he was wearing the same clothes as last night. He'd slept out there. I didn't say anything as he blushed and turned around.

"Either way, the others are probably waiting for us in Bill's strategy room or whatever he likes to call it. I think the latest was something like 'room Kenny is not allowed to touch anything in' or something like that."

I laughed. I could definitely see Bill calling it that. Kenny did seem to like to break Bill's things, whether it was on purpose or not. Now he had to keep his hands in his pockets.

I followed Chase toward the meeting room where they were going over the last of the plans to attack. Everyone was there plus the soldiers that were under

Bill's command. Since Malcolm wasn't in this world that often, all his men served under Bill unless he was present, or that was what I gathered. Anytime we were in Wonderland, Malcolm swiftly gave orders, and no one ever asked questions or back-talked him. He had such authority in this realm.

"We are going to split up to cover more area," Bill explained as he pointed at the map. "We will have five groups. I will go in from the forest, Melvin and Kenny can go in from the rose garden, Chase and David go in from the croquet area, and Malcolm and Alice can go in through the maze. Then when we each enter the castle, I will search the highest floor, Melvin and Kenny ground level, Chase and David on the lower levels, and Malcolm and Alice can check the basement and cells as that was where she was taken. White Rabbit, you stay here in case this is a trap and Morpheus is after the king and queen. Any questions?"

I raised my hand. "Most of the castle is in ruins, but there could be other areas that are still accessible besides the tower he took me in. Do we have a plan on how to sweep those?"

Bill nodded. "Yes. Once we are done with the tower, each team will go through the other areas to see if there are any hideouts. I have a feeling he will show himself before then, but we will regroup after the initial search and divide out the rest."

"That sounds good."

"Each unit will have twenty soldiers with them. It should be enough to overpower Morpheus even if he attacks. He might have been gathering his strength, but he is much weaker than when he was at the circus, and he won't catch us by surprise. I want you all to listen to your commanders carefully and stick together unless told otherwise."

Malcolm placed his hand on my shoulder. "It will be fine. See, we have a plan and there are a lot of us. There is no way he will win."

"Yeah. I guess you are right."

"Any other questions?" Bill asked.

Everyone was quiet, as if listening to see if anyone would come up with something. As time went on, no one said anything.

Bill clapped his hands. "Good, now we all need to suit up and get our weapons ready. Chase will then open portals to each area, and we will all go through to our destinations. If you have questions, ask your commander. Now let's go."

I followed Chase as he gathered his men. He went through the map of the maze and gave out a few copies to different men. I wished I had a map when I was running for my life earlier. Malcolm gave me a copy, and I realized there was almost a straight stretch through the maze to get through it. Life was so unfair.

Chase used his powers and started to make portals to the different locations. It was strange watching him work as he was able to do it with a movement of his hand. Bill used his strange device on his arm and was able to keep them open for everyone to pass through. This was it. We were doing this.

Malcolm took my hand, and we stepped through the portal.

Chapter 18

Even though it was daylight, the Heart Castle looked as eerie and forgotten as it had last time. Gray clouds filled the sky, just like they did in Oregon most days of the year, making the place look even more depressing. The maze stretched all the way up to the ruins of the castle, and my heart raced at the memory from the day before. I squeezed Malcolm's hand, trying to calm myself down. He was here this time—I wasn't alone.

After all the men stepped through the portal and it closed, I took a deep breath as Malcolm gathered himself to give orders.

"You five, start covering the northeast section, and you five search the southwest section. Mark where you have been so we can make sure every inch of this maze has been searched. The rest of you follow me as we go straight through to the other side and start searching the lower levels of the castle."

The men nodded and did as they were ordered. Ten men were left with us as we marched toward the castle. Each of them had a sword, ready to battle. I gulped, wondering what traps Morpheus could have set. It didn't seem like he had many men on his side other than whoever was pulling the strings. What if the person behind it all sent in reinforcements? Would we be able to match them?

Malcolm didn't say much as he led us through the maze. He seemed determined yet calm about all this. I wondered what was running through his mind and whether he knew his way through the maze. He didn't look at the map the entire time, which surprised me. It had been years since he set foot in the Heart Kingdom, or at least that was what I gathered. Could he really remember a maze as large as this after so much time?

"Why don't you check the map as you go?" I asked. "I mean, it's been a while, hasn't it?"

He shook his head. "I know this maze like the back of my hand. I used to hide in here from the queen's guards all the time. Including Kenny. Or sometimes with Kenny."

"How did that go?"

He shrugged. "He's a little loud, and that defeats the purpose of hiding."

I laughed. "That's what I figured. I couldn't imagine

trying to hide with him."

"I was originally trying to just hide by myself, but then he tagged along. He does that, if you haven't noticed."

"I've noticed. He's nice though."

"Yeah, he has that going for him, I suppose. And he's loyal, as long as you aren't evil. He wasn't very loyal to the Queen of Hearts, I can tell you that."

"Because of that tart?"

"Because of that tart…"

I giggled at the idea of Kenny stealing the queen's tart. I knew that, at the time, it had almost cost him his life, but the fact that it was centuries later and he always brought it up was rather funny.

We went forward more, and I looked down at my own map. "It feels like we are just zigzagging along."

Malcolm nodded. "The path through this maze is just a zigzag, or at least for the most part. People get the mindset that they need to move in a different direction in this maze when really it's a straight shot. It's simple enough that I still have it memorized even after all these years."

That made sense I supposed. We pressed farther, now halfway through the maze.

The maze was eerie, even more so than the corn maze at Fordyce Farm back in Salem during the night. I did not like going at night, but at least I knew, deep down, something couldn't hurt me there. Here, there could be anything.

As if on cue, there was a loud roar that felt like it shook the ground. I glanced at Malcolm, who looked as worried as I felt, which made me feel worse. He wasn't one to show fear.

"What direction did that come from?" he shouted at his men.

They all pointed in different directions. The roar echoed through the maze again, and each of them changed the direction where they were pointing. Comical, if it weren't for the fact that we were about to die.

Another roar echoed and Malcolm shook his head. I couldn't tell which way it was coming from either. It sounded as if it was coming from every direction. He grabbed my hand and turned back toward the way we were already heading. "Everyone just run!"

The fact that Malcolm would rather run than face whatever it was coming after us terrified me the most. He always seemed to be a man of action, and with there being twelve of us, why would just a creature be a threat? What was going on?

We ran farther through the maze with whatever was after us screaming and roaring. I still couldn't quite figure out which direction it was coming from but could also hear the snapping of rosebushes and hedges as it came closer.

Damn, I was happy that this thing didn't attack

when I was running from Morpheus. I would have been killed in an instant.

I wondered if the creature had been released by Morpheus or if it was just a coincidence. It was probably Morpheus, as it was perfect timing for him. I wondered if any of the others had to deal with creatures like this.

Screams of humans echoed the maze. Whatever it was must have found the other ten soldiers that had been sweeping the area. My heart ached, thinking about what could be happening for them. I noticed Malcolm was picking up the pace and trying even harder to get away.

The sound of loud galloping through the maze, snapping the hedges, became louder, and as I turned around, I found a large beast running straight toward us.

"What is that?" I screamed.

Malcolm let go of my hand and pulled out his sword. "It's a bandersnatch, and it seems we need to fight it here and now."

The creature was massive with large teeth and a face that almost appeared like a jaguar's. As it inhaled to roar again, its neck expanded like a pouch, and its roar sent us flying back. I quickly stood back up and pulled out my own sword. I had to help battle this thing. I wouldn't let it take any more lives.

Malcolm stood in front of everyone and readied his

sword. "Do not let the bandersnatch's claws or fangs touch you as they are venomous!"

The bandersnatch charged for us, swiping at the soldiers who were in front. They were able to block the attacks with their swords, but that didn't mean the force of the attack didn't send them backward. They were sent through the dead hedge, crashing into the pile of leaves. I hoped they didn't have to deal with the cuts from the thorns like I had.

Malcolm didn't waver as the bandersnatch came barreling toward us. He held up his sword as it slashed at him, blocking the claws before they were able to pierce his skin. I wanted to help, but after Malcolm saying the claws were venomous, I was afraid to get close. I didn't want to get near in fear that I would become its next victim.

Slashing at the creature, Malcolm was able to pierce its fur and skin. The creature let out a terrible scream, blowing us all back. I wondered how a creature could be so forceful with its roar like that and figured it had to have been because of its expanding neck.

Three of the soldiers tried to charge at the bandersnatch, but it simply kicked up its legs and jammed its back nails into two of the men. I ran toward the creature, swinging my sword at its throat. I was able to make a cut, and it tried to scream out, but the sound was a lot less powerful. My attack worked.

Except now I was face-to-face with the creature.

"Alice! Run!" Malcolm yelled as he came running toward me. I quickly did as he said and went back into the maze from the area this creature had cleared. Malcolm slashed at its side, but that didn't stop it from chasing after me.

There was no way I was going to be able to outrun this creature, especially since it was running through the hedges and I had to go around the thorns. It barreled at me like a large pumpkin shooting out of a canon. Nothing was going to stop it.

I had to fight it. It was my only chance. If I could hold it off until the others got here, then we would have a chance in defeating it.

Spinning around, I slashed at the creature's face. It backed away, shaking its head in frustration. It swiped at me, but I used my katana to block the blow. It hissed and spat, and I prayed that its venom wasn't in its saliva. It used more force with its paw and pushed me back.

I rolled across the ground, dropping my katana along the way. I peered up to find the bandersnatch ready to pounce. My katana was a few feet away, and if I wasn't fast enough, this thing was going to kill me. I scrambled as the creature started to move.

Then it let out a terrifying scream.

I gathered my katana and found Malcolm. He'd stabbed his sword through the leg of the creature. He pulled out the sword, and the creature growled and turned to him. Malcolm backed away as if egging the creature on, and it charged him.

"Malcolm!" I screamed but found I didn't need to worry. He was able to jump out of the way and make a swift cut, slicing off one of the bandersnatch's paws. The creature roared in pain and stumbled down. More men gathered around it. It snarled and snapped at the soldiers.

"Watch out for its mouth now!" Malcolm yelled, and the creature tried to bite the closest soldiers.

The creature tried to get up, but it was no use. Malcolm slashed at its other leg, and the creature couldn't move any longer. Blood soaked the ground below it, a grotesque smell wafting through the area. Malcolm, careful of the creature's mouth, stabbed his sword through the creature's stomach. It thrashed around, but Malcolm stabbed it again and again, blood splattering across his clothes. The creature struggled a little more and finally was silent. Malcolm had put it out of its misery, and out of ours. I glanced around to find six of the soldiers left from the ten we had been with. Had four really been killed by this creature? It was still early in this battle, and yet we had lost so many.

Malcolm turned to me and smiled, blood now splattered on his clothes. "Shall we get out of this maze?"

I nodded quickly as he wiped his sword off on the

fur of the bandersnatch. He put his sword back in its scabbard and held out his hand. I took it, ready to get out of there.

Malcolm didn't seem to show any signs of resentment for the creature or seemed to be bothered about his clothes. He didn't even stop to see how many men were left or to go back and see if he could save the others. He was more concerned about moving forward. Was it because he only saw them as dreams and not as important as say Davis and Melvin? Or was there something else?

Flashbacks to the Dark Forest came through my mind. I had found bones of all kinds, including humans. Had Malcolm killed them? And if so, why? Was it out of self-defense? Or had something else happened in that forest that I didn't want to find out?

Chapter 19

The moment we stepped outside the maze I felt a weight come off my chest. I didn't realize how much I hated that maze. Actually, I take that back. I hated it a lot.

The rest of the men swept the maze and were able to catch up with us as we spent some time battling that bandersnatch. It appeared that five more men had been killed by it, leaving eleven soldiers and Malcolm and me. I couldn't believe that we had lost almost half our group. It was sad, and I felt bad for those dreams. I wondered if they had families or if they were just soldiers. Could dreams be soldiers? It made sense as they were citizens of the kingdom and weren't characters from the book.

It sort of felt like they were expendable. I didn't like

that about this place. Even if they were just dreams, it didn't mean they weren't living people. I still didn't understand the details of this place, however, and there were pieces I didn't quite understand. Whether I would find those pieces was still up for debate. Hopefully I would get my answers before long. If not, I would demand them.

"Next up, the castle," Malcolm announced. "We will be exploring the basement. I am sure many of the other groups are already searching, granted they didn't have a random creature attack them as well. Be on the lookout for anything. It was apparent that Morpheus had sent that thing after us, and he could have something even worse waiting."

I gulped. I didn't want to think of what other creatures could be under his control. I wondered if the bandersnatch came from the Dark Forest. Seeing as how scary it was, the answer was probably yes. I was glad I didn't come across those when I was alone out there.

That being said, I wondered how he was able to control them or if he had simply let it loose to wreak its havoc. Either way, he had to have been keeping it captive somewhere. That, or whoever was pulling the strings was able to keep it tamed for him.

So maybe we could narrow it down to anyone in Wonderland who could tame beasts.

I made a mental note to bring that up to Malcolm

later. I believe I was onto something, and if Morpheus wouldn't reveal who was behind it all, it could be a start.

The tower that was left standing was a lot grander than I remembered, mainly because I wasn't as scared for my life. I mean, I still was, but a lot less with Malcolm standing next to me, and I wasn't alone with a madman pulling me down to the prison. It stood tall, unmoved by time itself. A lot of the building around it crumbled, and I wondered why it was the only thing remaining that stood against the test of time.

Perhaps it was just luck.

The stone was a faded red. Did the queen really love that color as much as the stories had mentioned? I supposed if someone was going to make her servants paint so many roses, she would want her castle to be red as well.

We entered and everything seemed to be frozen in time. Much of it was covered in a layer of dust, and I felt my nose start to itch as others had already started to search the rest of the castle. Dust filled the air, and I tried not to sneeze.

"The dungeon is this way." Malcolm gestured toward the stairway that led down. I could hear Kenny's voice down the hallway. I was glad to hear he was safe and sound. As I listened a little closer, I could hear him say something about tarts. I saw Malcolm roll his eyes, and he ushered me away.

"That man and tarts," Malcolm whispered.

"Maybe I should make him some after all this is over."

"No, you would only add to the problem."

I laughed a little. I probably would make him some but would have to give it to him outside of school as it would be embarrassing to make a new student teacher something like that. I wouldn't want others to get the wrong idea.

The stairs went on for longer than I remembered. My legs ached more than normal, probably from running all day the day before. I must have run for miles. Is this what Kate felt like every day? I didn't understand how she did it. She was amazing.

We finally got down to the dungeon level, and I stayed behind Malcolm as he slowly opened the door to peek inside. I didn't hear anything, and I wondered if Morpheus would really wait for us all the way down here. I was surprised he hadn't shown himself yet, as he wanted to battle so bad.

Malcolm pushed the door all the way open and pulled out his sword. I did the same, feeling stronger with the weight of my katana in my hands. The eleven soldiers each drew their weapons, ready to attack if any problem should arise.

The dungeon area was just like it was yesterday, except I wasn't in a cell. The door to the cell was still open, exactly how I'd left it. Had he come back in here after leaving last night? What if he had totally ditched me? Or whatever the noise was had killed him or took him somewhere?

What was going on?

Glancing over to Malcolm, he seemed to have the same concerns as I did. Where was Morpheus?

"This is where he took you?" Malcolm asked.

I nodded. "Yes. I was in that cell and was able to pick the lock. Then I stole his water and ran."

"And you said he left you here when he heard one of his alarms sound?"

"Yup."

"No dream would have ever come out here. And we all were on Earth; the king and queen were in the palace. Who could have come out here and where could he have gone?"

I glanced around. It really didn't look like he came back here, or if he did, he simply saw I was gone and then went out looking for me. "You don't think he is still here?"

Malcolm shook his head. "I think he would have shown his face by now. That, or…" He peered around. "Crap. Get down!"

He dove on top of me just as a loud, thunderous explosion rang through the dungeon. Dust and rubble filled my vision before I closed my eyes. I coughed as the sound seemed to stop, but the ringing in my ears made it difficult to tell. Echoes of another explosion made it down all the way to the level we were at. He had booby-trapped the entire area. I guess if you wanted to survive and defeat so many soldiers, you would resort to such cowardly tactics.

"Malcolm," I called out. "Are you all right?"

He slowly stood up and held out his hand. "I will manage." He bent down and grabbed his hat and dusted it off. "Are you fine?"

"Yes, thanks to you. How did you know?"

"I saw the bomb right before it went off. My guess is he waited until all of us were in the castle."

I glanced around. I saw one man with his legs sticking out from under the rubble. "We have to help him!"

Malcolm grabbed my wrist. "The other soldiers will find the survivors. We first need to see if we can find a way out of here. If I'm not mistaken, he had many bombs scattered around, and it could have blocked our exit."

I nodded as some of the soldiers started to move the rubble. I wanted to help and make sure they were all okay, but Malcolm had a point—we needed to find a way out of here.

Grabbing my katana from the ground, I followed Malcolm as he went back into the stairwell. We climbed up what felt like the equivalent of three flights and found that it indeed had been closed off from the debris of a bomb.

"Great. We are stuck here until we can move this or pray that Chase is fine and comes down here." Malcolm started to pick up some of the broken brick and move it.

I put away my katana and began to help him, trying not to think about the fact we were trapped here and that our friends could have met a far worse fate than this. My hands were shaking as I moved the rock, and I did my best to steady my breath, but it did nothing. I knelt down and cradled my legs.

Malcolm bent down and placed his hand on my back. "It's okay, we will find a way out of here."

Tears rolled down my cheeks. "But it is my fault that you all came down here. He set me up, and I have caused so much death and destruction."

"It would have happened either way, Alice. Morpheus needs to be stopped. All the soldiers know this and knew they could lose their lives on this mission. It isn't your fault."

"But what about the others? We don't know if they are alive or what. Chase could be…"

"He's not dead. If a little explosion like that could kill him, he would have been dead a long time ago. Believe me, I've tried killing him myself multiple times." He laughed a little.

I didn't know what to make of him saying that. I had seen them fight, but to say he tried to kill him was something completely different.

Taking a few deep breaths, I nodded. "Okay. I'm fine. I'm sorry about that."

"It's understandable, Alice. You have been through a lot these past two days."

It definitely felt like more than two days had gone by. I helped Malcolm with the rubble, but as we kept moving stuff, it felt as if it wasn't helping at all. How much had broken and fallen? Could the rest of the tower have completely collapsed? I tried not to think about it and kept helping Malcolm. I wondered if we were actually making a difference or if he was just trying to distract me from the fact we were trapped here.

I felt a hand touch my shoulder and I shrieked. I turned to find Chase standing there, dust covering his hair and clothes but otherwise okay. He wrapped his arms around me.

"Alice. Thank goodness you are okay."

"Am I just chopped liver?" Malcolm commented, although I wasn't sure if it was toward me or Chase.

Chase gave him a look. "No, I like chopped liver more than I like you."

"Whatever. What happened up there? Is everyone okay?"

"The commanders are all fine, although Bill took a pretty big blow to the head, and Kenny took him back to the castle. I transported the wounded soldiers back as well. We only have about twenty left of the original one hundred, plus whoever survived down here. This is the last area I have transported to."

Malcolm bit his lip. I didn't like those numbers and hoped most were just wounded and not dead.

"Go take the wounded down there to the castle along with Alice and then come back to take me up to the main floor. I have a feeling I know where to find Morpheus."

My eyes widened. "No, I don't want to go back! I want to help fight!"

Malcolm placed his hands on my shoulders. "Alice, I can't fight while worrying about you. I thought I could, but I just can't. I will be able to move more freely around and find this bastard without you here. Do you understand?"

I slowly nodded. I did understand, but that didn't mean I liked it.

Chase grabbed my hand. "Come on Alice, we need to go get those men real quick."

I followed Chase down to where the wounded were. Chase made a portal, and we were able to help them all together. I stepped through the portal and was back in the castle. Dozens of soldiers lay in the sick bay, or whatever it was called. Most were covered in blood and I tried to look away, afraid what might have happened to them.

As Chase began to return to the portal to the Heart Castle, I grabbed his wrists. "Can you promise me something?"

"What is it?"

"I want you to take Malcolm where he wants to go, and then I want you to come back and get me."

"Alice, he said…"

I shook my head. "No, I must help end this. I am Alice—I am the key to Wonderland, remember? I will be able to stop him. I don't care what Malcolm says."

Chase frowned but then finally nodded. "Fine. I'll come get you. Just wait right here."

With that, he left me standing there. I took a deep breath and prayed he would keep his word.

Chapter 20

I waited for Chase, my worry increasing as every second passed. Would he come back for me? Or would he do what Malcolm said and leave me there. Supposedly Malcolm knew where Morpheus would be hiding, but I didn't know why.

Seeing all these soldiers in the sick bay also didn't help my worry. There were fewer with Malcolm now, and anything could happen. Would my friends be fine? Would any more soldiers get injured?

Suddenly Chase appeared in front of me and grabbed my hand. "Hurry before anyone notices."

I nodded and let him transport me back to wherever the rest were. When we arrived, I realized where we were.

"This isn't inside the castle—this is the outskirts of

the Dark Forest."

Chase nodded. "Yeah… apparently Malcolm thinks Morpheus is somewhere inside. He split off from the rest, and they are scouring the forest. But for some reason Malcolm didn't let any of the soldiers join him."

"What? Why? I thought he said it was better to have numbers?"

Chase shrugged. "I never know how that man thinks. I just know that he honestly believes Morpheus is out there."

I stared out into the forest, reliving what had happened just the day before. I gulped.

"It's up to you, Alice. You don't have to go out there. I can take you back…"

I shook my head. "No, I have to help. Morpheus used me, and I want to see him stopped once and for all. I will help."

"Then we better get going and catch up. There's a lot to go through."

I took a deep breath as we stepped into the woods. "You know this place well, right?"

"Yup, used to spend a lot of my time out here. Back when the queen cast me out. And to get away from the Duchess."

"Why did you want to get away from her?"

Chase sighed. "Many reasons. She can be a little much. And she acts innocent, but she really just kisses the ass of any person in power. She will do anything to keep her status, and usually that anything involved me. But that was the past, and I was freed once Alice destroyed the Red and White Kingdom. I have been free ever since."

I wanted to ask about the things he did, but it sounded like he didn't want to go into too much detail.

"Well, I am glad you are free, and I hope you can stay that way. I like the current you."

His tail swayed back and forth. "Thanks. You are probably the only one who thinks that."

I wanted to tell him he was wrong, but after the argument Malcolm and I had about him, I knew it was true. Whatever happened when he was with the Duchess still rubbed the others the wrong way.

And whatever happened in the Dark Forest made Chase hate Malcolm.

Was that why Morpheus hid in the Dark Forest and why Malcolm went off on his own? The Dark Forest seemed to be Malcolm's domain, so why would Morpheus risk it? Unless he wanted to taunt Malcolm, which would explain why Malcolm left the group.

He knew Morpheus had set this up just for him and decided to face him alone.

Even if that were the case, it didn't make sense why Malcolm would do this. It wasn't like the others didn't know his past and the things that happened there, and I was supposed to be back at the palace. No, Malcolm had other things going through his mind.

We entered through the singing flowers barrier that kept the creatures of the Dark Forest from escaping and most people out. I put my hands to my ears and tried to ignore their sweet music. Chase led us away from them, and I uncovered my ears.

"So, which way did Malcolm go?"

Chase frowned a little. "Are you sure that's where you want to go? I mean, everyone else could probably use backup too…"

I raised an eyebrow. "Why are you hesitant to find Malcolm out here?"

"He gets a little… dark… when he's in the Dark Forest." He smirked a little. "See what I did there?"

"Chase…"

"He used to be the queen's executioner, all right? The queen would send people out here for him to kill. It was his job, so you can't really judge him for it. He didn't really have a choice, but after a while, so many killings sort of eat at you. You can turn cold, and that is what happened with Malcolm." Chase looked away. "I shouldn't have been the one to tell you that, but I am just letting you know. He is used to being on his own and hunting people. He will be fine."

The queen's executioner? It made sense after everything that I had witnessed and how everyone acted around him. It was strange to think of him having such a morbid job, but if I were honest, no one in Wonderland who had a role had hands that were clean. It sounded like Chase had done things similar, and the rest were in the army—their hands were covered in blood as well.

It scared me, if I were honest. These people I considered friends had probably killed many men throughout the centuries they had been alive. But was that any different than the veterans in my own world? They did what they had to do, and no one should be ashamed of that.

But they also shouldn't have to face those demons alone.

"Let's go to Malcolm. He shouldn't do this alone."

Chase sighed. "He's going to be so pissed at me."

I grinned. "Isn't he always?"

"That's… fair. Okay, follow me. I can track him in this forest… and am probably the only one who can."

We walked through the forest for what felt like an hour. It was funny to watch Chase sniff the air like a cat as he was tracking Malcolm.

"Couldn't you track Morpheus like that though?"

Chase shook his head. "He uses some kind of magic to mask his scent. It's been annoying. Malcolm, however, has either never tried or I have known him for too long that I can easily pick it up. He's close though. We will have to try to be quiet so he doesn't know we are here."

"Wouldn't we want him to know we are here? Otherwise he might almost attack us if he notices something is following."

"That is definitely fair. But we also don't want him to get angry with us. We will just stay a bit out and get closer if I sense he needs help."

"That sounds like a plan."

Chase kept sniffing around as I followed him, peering around. Moss covered everything as far as the eye could see. I wondered how long this had gone untouched for it to have spread like this. I knew a few people who collected different types moss and they would have had a field day out here, other than the constant fear of getting attacked by creatures and such. There was also the fact that it could be poisonous or something. I mean, it was the Dark Forest after all.

The fog covered the ground up to my knees, which always freaked me out. I was careful to step where Chase stepped. He didn't seem to mind the fog, but I hated not being able to see the ground I was stepping on, especially since it was soft and squishy. So far, I hadn't heard any creatures roaring in the distance. I didn't know if that was because it was still somewhat early in the day or if it was because the others had battled them, or they didn't like how many people were in here and were hiding. Either way, I was both happy about it and a little concerned.

"He's just up ahead. We should probably stay back

here. But I think if we go up in this tree, we will be able to see him."

I looked up the tree. I did not like heights at all. I let out a sigh. "Fine, whatever. Just help me up and promise me you won't let me fall."

"I promise. It's just like dance, Alice. You aren't afraid of falling when any of the guys are lifting you up."

"That's a lot closer to the ground than a tree."

"It's all the same. Just don't fall."

"Yeah, easy for you to say..."

I started to climb the tree, and as I got to the first large branch, my boots slipped on the moss. I almost screamed when Chase caught me.

"The goal is to be quiet, Alice. Weren't you listening to me earlier?"

I shot him a look and gathered myself. I was able to make it to the next branch, and I peered out to see what I could see. The forest was dense, of course, but we were on the outskirts of a clearing.

The clearing that had the table with the teacups.

Chase climbed up next to me and looked down. "Yeah, that's where I figured we were."

"This is the Mad Hatter's Tea Party, right?"

He nodded. "Yeah. This is where Malcolm used to live. From here, he would get the orders from the queen and would begin his hunt."

"So what's he doing here?" I asked.

Chase gestured to look forward. "Morpheus."

I peered around the hanging moss and found that Morpheus was sitting at the table as if waiting for Malcolm. Malcolm stood at the edge of the opening, glaring at Morpheus.

"Malcolm, it took you long enough to find me." Morpheus gestured around. "I figured you would have loved to come back home."

"This isn't my home. I was forced to live here."

Morpheus chuckled. "Right. Forced."

"Don't try to spin things. It won't work on me."

"I'm not spinning anything, Malcolm. I have been inside your mind—you miss this part of yourself. It's something you have always accepted."

"Is that right?"

"It is. You liked being the executioner. It gave you a thrill—to be able to hunt in a kill-or-be-killed scenario. Your role before that was rather boring, wasn't it? This gave you something to look forward to each and every day. The March Hare and the Dormouse also liked to play these games, but not as much as you."

Malcolm didn't move but glared at Morpheus. I just watched, afraid of what Morpheus might do.

I whispered into Chase's ear. "Shouldn't we help him?"

Chase shook his head but didn't say anything. I turned back to watch the scene unfold in front of me.

"What do you want, Morpheus? It's not like you can

make me into one of your minions. What is your purpose of causing so much destruction in the Heart Castle to only dare me out here?"

"Isn't it obvious? I want you to give in to the games you used to play."

Malcolm let out a small laugh. "Even if I killed you right now, it would have nothing to do with my previous role. I would kill you because of all the trouble you have caused."

"Is that so?"

"Besides, you have lost and we have won. You won't be dying, because we need you to tell us who is pulling your strings."

Morpheus let out a laugh. "You think I am just a puppet? You better think again."

"We know you are working with someone. You are not powerful on your own—at least not with what stunts you have been pulling lately. You have someone on the inside, and I am going to find out who exactly that is."

Malcolm pulled out his sword. "Now stand up and put your hands behind your head."

Morpheus stood up and did as ordered. "You know, Malcolm, it would be a shame if your beautiful Alice ever found out about the man you used to be."

"She doesn't need to know. That was ancient history and has nothing to do with the man I am today."

"You think so? You think you no longer kill in cold

blood?"

Malcolm grabbed Morpheus's wrists and placed cuffs on them. "Nope. I am not that person."

Morpheus looked up straight at Chase and I. Chase let out a slight gasp.

"Oh no. Alice, we need to get down there."

Chase helped me down the tree, and I could hear the conversation go on.

"What if Alice was here, Malcolm, watching? What if I unloaded all your secrets?"

"She's not here. She is back at the palace."

"Listen, Hatter, do you not hear the rustling in the trees?"

Malcolm was silent as we climbed down. Chase reached the ground and helped me down the rest of the way. We stepped out into the clearing. Malcolm's eyes widened, and then he glared at Chase.

"I told you to leave her behind!"

I stepped in front of Chase. "It wasn't his fault. I ordered him to bring me out here. I wanted to help capture Morpheus and take him in."

Malcolm glared at Chase, and Morpheus started laughing.

"Oh, Malcolm. Your worst fear has now been realized, hasn't it? Dear little Alice heard the truth of what you were."

I shook my head. "It doesn't matter. As he said, that was in the past and it was his role—he couldn't do anything about it."

Another laugh. "Then how about you hear the truth. The Mad Hatter used to bring his victims here. He used to—"

With a swift motion of his arm, Malcolm cut off Morpheus's head.

Chapter 21

"What did you do that for? Malcolm! We needed him to get the information of the person behind it all!" Chase shouted as I just stared at the body that was once Morpheus. It collapsed to the ground right at Malcolm's feet.

Malcolm looked down at the body as if it were just some piece of garbage. "He wouldn't have told us the truth. He would have led us on one wild-goose chase after another. It will be easier to find the truth without him."

Chase shook his head as he stepped up to Malcolm. "That wasn't your call! The right thing to do would have been to let the king and queen decide!"

"I will not take crap from you, Chase. You don't know anything about rules."

"Screw you, Malcolm! I am sick of you thinking you are righteous after everything you have done, meanwhile treating me like I am a scoundrel. I have done a lot less horrible things than you have!"

Malcolm straightened his arm and placed the sword under Chase's throat. "Shut up, cat! I can no longer deal with your insolence! Just leave!"

Chase pulled out his own sword. "No! I am done taking orders from you." Chase held up his sword. "If you want to fight, then be my guest!"

The two of them stared at each other, ready to go into an all-out battle. I was frozen there, still in shock that Morpheus had been killed so swiftly. After everything, Malcolm had executed him on the spot. Did he deserve it? Was this a just ending?

I was able to come back to the present and pulled out my own katana. "That is enough! No more death today, please!" Tears were streaming down my face. "I just want to go back now, okay? All of us—together."

Chase and Malcolm glared at each other for another moment, then Malcolm sighed. "Fine." He put his sword away. "We will need to go find the rest of the crew. We had a spot where we were going to meet up with everyone. Let's head that way."

Lowering his sword, Chase kept it out and watched as Malcolm turned and started into the forest again.

"Come on, Alice. I will feel better if you were at my side through this forest. There are a lot of monsters out here—ones that not even Chase could defeat."

I glanced at Chase, who simply nodded to go. I hurried after Malcolm and watched as Chase didn't follow. I worried keeping him there by himself, but he didn't seem to want to go near Malcolm. Chase knew this forest—it wouldn't be a problem for him to get out.

Malcolm grabbed my hand and kissed it. "I am glad no harm came to you because of Chase's mistake."

"Again, I asked him to bring me."

"And if he had any brains, he wouldn't have listened."

I peered up into Malcolm's eyes. They were soft and sweet now—completely different than just moments ago. Was this the real Malcolm, or was it the one who killed so easily?

"What's wrong?" Malcolm asked as we had been standing there for a few moments.

I shook my head. "Nothing."

"We both know that isn't true. You fear me now, don't you?"

"It's not that exactly... I just don't understand why you killed him or how you killed him so easily."

Malcolm let out a breath. "This is why I didn't want you here. I knew he was going to goad me like that. But you know as well as I that he wouldn't have told the truth—we would just have been sent on a wild-goose chase. As for my swiftness... I'm sorry you had to see that. I just couldn't…"

He looked away. The demons of his past still did haunt him, even if he tried to always have a calm demeanor. "I just don't want you to have anything to do with that part of my life. It was a dark time for me. I hate being in these woods as it reminds me of all those years. Melvin and Davis shared the same fight as I had, although I bet they would have been able to keep a better demeanor than me."

I wasn't sure how to respond. I placed my hand on his cheek. "It's okay. Just… just stop taking it out on Chase, okay? He was just trying to help."

Malcolm frowned. "No, that cat was in this mess deeper than I was. He tries to act like he is innocent, and that is what makes it worse."

I found it ironic that they both had said the same thing about each other. "I just don't want to see him dead, okay? He's my friend now—we are all friends now. If you don't want me to be a part of that past, you have to forgive him as well. You can't have it both ways."

He furrowed his brow. He knew I had a point. Taking in a deep breath, he turned back around and started toward where we needed to go. "Yeah, I guess. I will try."

"Thank you."

He held my hand as we ventured through the forest. I cared for Malcolm, and I knew that there was a lot about Wonderland I didn't understand and may never understand, but I still wasn't sure how I felt about it all.

And the fact was that I still didn't know what role I played in all of it.

After two hours of walking, we found Bill and Kenny near the edge of the Dark Forest. I could almost hear the flowers in the distance. As we stepped up to them, Melvin and Davis also appeared from the forest.

"Malcolm! Did you find him?" Bill asked as everyone gathered around. He looked over at me. "Alice! Where did you come from?"

"Chase went against my orders, of course, and brought her here. He's probably outside the forest waiting for us to take us back to the palace. As for Morpheus..." He paused, as if trying to find his wording. "He is dead. There was an argument, and I let my emotions get the better of me."

Everyone was silent. I felt a bit awkward, not sure what to say. Maybe I shouldn't have come. Would Malcolm still have killed Morpheus if I hadn't shown? Would he still be in as much trouble as he was now?

"We will be having a long talk after we get back," Bill commented. "You knew we needed him."

"I know. I am sorry. But he would have just lied and wasted our time."

"He would have revealed something at least. Now

we have no idea where to start."

"But we don't have to worry that someone would release him or get to Alice. We are probably at the same spot we would be at either way."

Kenny jumped in. "He's gone. There isn't anything we can do. As Malcolm said, killing him will bring more safety to Alice for the time being. Now we can just focus on finding clues." He started jumping up and down. "Mystery! I do love a good mystery!"

Davis squeaked. "At least no one else got hurt."

Melvin nodded in agreement. "Yeah. Now let's just get out of here. I don't want to be in this creepy place any longer."

Bill stared at Malcolm a moment longer, then turned toward the field of flowers. "Right. The battle is over and we need to get out of here before the light dims any more."

We made our way through the field of flowers. I counted all the soldiers that were with us, and it seemed that the twenty who had entered were still all fine. The fact that we didn't lose any more people made my heart happy.

As Malcolm guessed, Chase was already out of the Dark Forest and ready to take us back to the palace. He and Malcolm didn't look at each other, and I tried to ignore the awkwardness. I felt bad for both of them as they misunderstood each other greatly. They could be good friends if they didn't let the past affect that.

We stepped through the portal and were back in front of the palace. I smiled at the sight, knowing that it was finally over—or at least the battle with Morpheus. I knew there was still a battle to be fought and, as Kenny said, a mystery to solve.

But at least I didn't have to worry about him appearing in my dreams.

Malcolm grabbed my hand, and I looked over at him and found that he looked a bit worried. I wondered if it was because now he had to tell the queen and king what he had done. I wouldn't look forward to that conversation either. It already seemed that Bill was pissed.

Bill clapped his hands. "All right. Soldiers, you are dismissed. You can either go home or visit your colleagues in the sick bay. Commanders, follow me as we need to report to the king and queen. Since this battle didn't go as planned and we weren't able to capture Morpheus, they are going to want us to report individually to check our stories."

Malcolm bit his lip. This was not going to go well for him, especially with Chase saying what he'd seen.

And I would have to say what I witnessed as well.

Now I was worried and didn't want to throw Malcolm under the bus. I understand why he did it. It was wrong, of course, in some ways, but this was also someone who wanted to destroy all of Wonderland. If Malcolm didn't kill him, he still could have caused more destruction.

Bill led us into the palace. Everyone seemed to have been waiting for us, which made sense. I felt a bit subconscious as everyone was staring at us and whispering. I looked back at Chase, whose ears were down, and he was looking away. I wished I knew what he was thinking and hoped that our group friendship wouldn't be harmed after what happened in the forest.

We came upon the throne room, and Bill turned to everyone. "I will talk to them first. Everyone wait outside, and you will be called in one at a time."

Bill left us, and most everyone sat down on the floor. Malcolm sat against the wall and banged his head softly. I stroked his hand with my thumb but didn't say anything. I wondered what his punishment would be or if he would even receive one.

Chase lay on the ground and stared at the ceiling, like a cat would when it was bored. It sort of made me smile. Melvin and Davis were quiet as well, knowing they would have to tell them what they thought happened and how Malcolm wanted to go out on his own. Kenny was even quiet, which surprised me. He was pacing back and forth though, which was the only noise in the hallway.

A few minutes went by and Bill came out. "Malcolm, you are first."

Malcolm stood up and went inside. Bill went with him and was probably taking notes as he was the lead commander out of all of them. After the door closed, Chase got up and walked over to me.

"It will be fine. He won't be scolded too bad. I probably will get in more trouble having brought you."

"Thank you, by the way. I wanted to help finish this even if I didn't do much, or anything really. If I had to wait, I would have been worrying about you all, and I don't know what I would have done. Except now..."

"He would have killed him either way. Morpheus would have just found something else to piss Malcolm off with, and he would have ended him. It was all part of Morpheus's plan."

"I suppose so. But still, I feel partially responsible. I just hope nothing bad comes of it."

"Cheer up. We will figure out who was pulling the strings, and Wonderland will be peaceful once again."

I bit my lip. "But then what?"

He cocked his head to the side. "What do you mean?"

"I mean... then what about me?"

Chase frowned and looked away. I was about to ask again when the door opened.

"Chase," Bill said as Malcolm stepped out, holding his head high. "You are next."

Chase smiled to me. "Don't worry, Alice, this is all formality. No one will be in trouble. We will head back home in no time."

I watched as Chase and Malcolm passed each other

without saying a word or exchanging glances. Malcolm took a seat next to me, took off his top hat, and leaned his head on my shoulder. The door closed behind Chase, and I waited for when I would be called in next.

Chapter 22

A good hour passed as we sat outside, each awaiting our turns. Everyone had gone in except for me. I was last. I didn't know how I felt about that, as I was filled with worry and fear. Currently Kenny was inside, and who knew how long that would take, as Kenny could take quite some time to tell a story. Then again, he seemed to understand the importance of this meeting.

The door opened and I jumped up. Kenny came walking out and gave me a little smile. "Seems you are next, Alice. But don't worry, you won't get into any trouble. They just want you to tell them what happened."

I nodded. Malcolm stood up and gave me a kiss on my cheek. "Just tell the truth. We each already have."

It felt strange that he was being so sweet to me when

I was about to go in there to tell them he had killed the person we were supposed to capture alive. I stepped inside to find the king and queen sitting at their throne. The queen's kimono was covered in stars today, with a mixture of blue and yellow. The king's was similar, except it was black and white. It always seemed his matched hers but was monochromatic, which I thought was beautiful. The White Rabbit stood next to Bill, awaiting my story. He appeared tired as they had been going through everyone's stories. I bowed to them all.

"Alice, I presume you know why you are here?" the queen asked.

I glanced over to Bill, who nodded. I turned back to the king and queen. "Yes. You want me to state what I witnessed during the battle."

"And don't leave any detail out."

I took a breath. "We were to search the maze, which we did. Malcolm had ten of the men sweep the maze while the rest of us went straight through it to the castle. Once we were about halfway through, a bandersnatch attacked. A few men died from the venom, but we were able to defeat the creature and move on.

"Once we got to the castle, we went straight to the lower level where the dungeon awaited. Once there, we searched and Malcolm realized there was a bomb. The bomb went off and we took cover. I assume there were bombs all through the tower, causing many casualties. Malcolm and I tried to see if we could get out through the stairs, but it was blocked. We started moving the rubble until Chase appeared. Malcolm had to calm me down as well because I was afraid we were stuck and, due to the casualties, worried about the others.

"Malcolm then told Chase to bring me back here, which he did. I, however, forced Chase to come back and get me once Malcolm figured out the next plan of action."

"Forced him?" the White Rabbit asked. "How did you force him?"

I fiddled with the sleeve of my shirt. "I just... asked him I suppose. He came back for me and told me that everyone who was left went into the Dark Forest as that is where Malcolm believed Morpheus would be."

"How did he know that?" He inquired.

I shook my head. "Chase never said. My conclusion was that Morpheus wanted to get under Malcolm's skin and Malcolm figured that out."

The king cleared his throat. "What happened in the Dark Forest?"

"I asked Chase to find Malcolm since he said Malcolm went on his own to find Morpheus. Chase was able to track Malcolm, and we found him in a clearing. Chase and I hid in the trees and watched as Morpheus taunted Malcolm."

"What did Morpheus say?" the queen asked.

I shrugged. "I can't remember all of it, but it had to do with his job as an executioner for the Queen of Hearts. It was clear that Morpheus knew we were there, and when Chase figured that out, we climbed down and went to help Malcolm. Morpheus then tried to go into detail of what Malcolm had done as an executioner and then…" I paused and took a deep breath. The image was still crystal clear in my mind. "He killed Morpheus before he could reveal anything."

Bill was frowning but didn't say anything. The queen and king seemed to sit on that information for a moment.

"What happened after that?" the White Rabbit inquired.

I didn't know if I should mention the fight Malcolm and Chase had gotten into. It wasn't that big of a deal, but they both could get in a lot of trouble for it. Did they tell the king and queen about it? "Chase and Malcolm argued, and then I went with Malcolm to find the others and Chase went ahead to where he would open a portal." Before they could inquire any more, I went on. "It wasn't Malcolm's fault. Morpheus would have said anything to get under his skin. He shouldn't be punished for that. If I wasn't there, it could have gone differently. All this is my fault, not theirs."

The queen smiled. "Dear Alice, although I know you have a point, and your heart is where it should be, there is still the fact that not one but two of my commanders disobeyed direct orders. This isn't something that I can just ignore. Don't worry, their punishment won't be anything severe, but they still need to realize what they did was wrong and learn from it. They are too valuable to do anything else. We need them to find the traitor among us, whether it be another dream or a person with a role."

I nodded. I wasn't going to argue with her any longer as I knew her mind was made up.

"Now, please step outside while I discuss with the king what we should do."

Bill escorted me out to the hallway where everyone waited. I tried to keep a brave face, but I was afraid what they might make Chase and Malcolm do.

Bill clapped his hands, which he seemed to do right before making orders. It must have been his way to get everyone's attention. "For now, you all can retire to your rooms. I will come get you Malcolm and Chase when the king and queen decide." He checked his watch. "We will need to catch the bus soon on Earth, so it won't be too long."

We all turned to head to our rooms, and I prayed for the best scenario possible.

About thirty minutes passed when I heard voices outside my door. I cracked it open a little to find Bill talking to Chase and Malcolm as he led them down the hallway. Chase's ear twitched when he heard my door, but he didn't look back. After they disappeared around the corner, I stepped into the hallway to find Davis, Melvin, and Kenny were already following. I smiled a little.

"I see Alice is as worried as we are." Kenny laughed.

Melvin shook his head. "We really shouldn't—it's not like it's going to be that big of a punishment. Bill knows as well as us that we need them to find the insider."

I nodded. "Yeah, the queen said that to me as well."

"But that doesn't mean we shouldn't go and support them," Davis said as he nodded forward. "We should be there when they come out."

We traveled toward the throne room and waited outside. Kenny kept putting his ear to the door as if listening for any voices. He cursed as he stepped away. "I can't hear a bloody thing!"

I stared down the hallway. It seemed as if no servants wanted to come near this area with everything going on. I sighed as I awaited the verdict.

The doors to the throne room opened and Chase and Malcolm stepped out, both of them distraught, but Chase looked more sick than anything.

"Well?" Melvin asked. "What did they decide?"

Chase placed his face in his hands. "I have to clean Kenny's room for a year."

Kenny's hands went up in triumph. "Yes!"

Chase shook his head. "I can't believe this. Bill just

didn't want to deal with your dirty room, did he? So he is making me clean it."

Malcolm didn't say anything as he walked over toward me. He wrapped his arms around me. "I'm sorry."

"What?" I asked. "What is it?"

"I… I have to cut back my time spent on Earth. The king and queen think it would be best if I used my efforts to search here more than protect you. Melvin, Davis, and Chase will still go to school with you, but as of today, I no longer will be there."

My heart felt as if it dropped to my stomach. This wasn't fair. I mean… There really wasn't any reason for him to be at school with me any longer, and he really was needed back here, but that would mean I wouldn't get to hang out and lunches would be without him.

It could be worse, I told myself. He could have had a lot worse punishment.

I nodded. "It's fine. I mean, you need to protect Wonderland too. And I can always visit here, and I mean, we have more fun here."

Malcolm kept his arms around me. "Yeah, I suppose we do. I am just a bit bummed."

"Wait, Malcolm," Kenny commented. "Does that mean Bill and I won't be at your school any longer?"

"That's what Bill said."

"That's not fair. I really wanted to read about *Huckleberry Finn* and all the tarts."

Melvin put his hand on Kenny's shoulder. "We already told you—there are no tarts in that story."

"Right! Then I don't really care."

I cared, however. I was starting to get used to them all at school. It was a lot of fun and much more entertaining. Now I no longer had the person I cared about with me.

This really blew. But in the back of my mind, I knew it couldn't have lasted forever. In fact, there was still the matter of what Morpheus said about when I turned seventeen and how I would no longer be able to come to Wonderland.

"I will still come back today, however," Malcolm said. "As me just randomly disappearing would be a little strange."

"That's fair." I smiled. "Maybe we could do something after school."

"We have dance, remember?" Chase commented.

I frowned. "Right. Well, maybe after dance?"

Bill shook his head. "No, he needs to come straight here."

"Oh. Well, I'll come back here later this weekend then." I smiled. "We will figure something out."

Malcolm smiled, but it seemed empty, as if it was just duct tape on a bigger problem. He was thinking about the same thing I was and how there would be a point where I needed to choose.

Bill clapped his hands. "Well, we better get back to

Earth. Everyone go change into what you were wearing when you left, and we shall head out."

I slapped my hand on my forehead. My clothes were completely ruined. What the heck was I going to wear?

Chapter 23

We all stepped through the portal to find the Rose Garden exactly how we left it. The water fountain that Morpheus used to pull me through stood next to me and I quickly hoped away from it. I knew he was gone, but I really didn't want to get close to it. I took in a deep breath, the crisp spring air filled with rose-scent calmed me down. It felt strange that over a day had gone by, but it had been merely minutes in this world.

Time was relative.

I ended up wearing the dress that the farmer's wife gave me. It was completely different than my normal style, but I liked it. I would just have to say that I had gotten wet in a puddle and had this in my backpack for a dinner with my family later. It made sense and I felt cute in it, which caused me to be more confident in my lie.

We headed toward where the bus was and found that the rest of the class was getting in the bus. Perfect timing. We got in after everyone, but still managed to get seats in the back. It was funny how even if there was no seating arrangement, that students would sit where they always sat. People like to feel familiar with their surroundings, I supposed.

No one made a comment about my dress, which was fair because I forgot I was invisible to most people. It made little stuff like this easier to deal with. But at the same time, it stung a bit.

I collapsed in the seat, glad that everything was finally over. Malcolm took a seat next to me and I leaned my head on his shoulder. My hear heart knowing that I would be enjoying school with him any longer. It didn't seem fair that the rest got to stay, but I was glad that I wasn't being left completely alone, as I still wanted to be involved with Wonderland. Maybe the King and Queen would change their mind and he could come back.

Or we would find the person behind everything and he could come back because Wonderland was safe again.

But if that were the case, then they wouldn't need me any longer. When that happens, I will be all alone if they leave me. I didn't want to live life here without them, but I also didn't want to leave everything here.

There had a way to do both, right? Wonderland couldn't just disappear from my life like that.

Except that's how every anime ended—the person went back to the real world and had to leave it all behind. Especially otomes.

I glanced up at Malcolm who had his eyes shut. He was probably as tired as I was after the long battle. I peered around to find the rest trying to get some rest except Chase, who was looking out the window. He seemed worried, but I wasn't sure as to why. Was it because of everything that had happened with Malcolm? Or was it simply because he had to clean Kenny's room?

The hour went by and we were finally back at school. The bus let us all out and Malcolm and I went to a more secluded place where we could talk—a place my sister wouldn't happen across.

"So…" I began.

"I'm sorry it ended this way."

I shook my head. "No, it probably would have ended this way anyway since you would be needed back there to help with the search."

He shrugged. "I suppose, but how it happened wasn't very… gentleman-like." He smiled. "I'm sorry you had to see that side of me."

I didn't know what to say. I watched him kill someone because he didn't want that man to reveal his past. Even though that man was responsible for many deaths, it was still sort of... odd. Part of me understood, mainly after all the anime and books I read, but actually witnessing it was a whole different things.

I grabbed the sleeve of his coat. "There is something I wanted to talk about, before you go, since it might be a bit and we are alone now."

His face turned into instant worry. "What is it?"

"In Wonderland... when I was taken by Morpheus, he mentioned that I wouldn't be able to come to Wonderland once I reached seventeen. Is that true?"

Malcolm bit his lip. "Can we discuss this some other time?"

"No, I want answers now, Malcolm. Please, tell me the truth."

"It's complicated. I mean... I suppose that was how long the other Alice had."

I couldn't believe what I was hearing. Was he really going to be all nonchalant about it? "Were you going to tell me?"

"... Eventually."

"I... Malcolm, why didn't you say anything earlier? We could have figured something out. We could find a way where I could stay or maybe even travel between the two worlds."

"There isn't a way. I have looked into it for many years. There is no way for Alice to travel after she turns seventeen."

I couldn't believe what I was hearing. He had already searched? As in… "You wanted the other Alice to be able to come back?"

He didn't answer, which answered my question entirely. I knew he had feelings for her, but hearing how hard he tried for her, and how he kept ignoring the subject when it came to me, was starting to bother me more and more.

"Well then, what if I stayed in Wonderland and never came back here? What then?"

Malcolm stared at me for a long while then finally shook his head. "I won't allow it."

I couldn't believe what I was hearing. "You won't allow it? What does that mean?"

"I mean, I don't want you to stay in Wonderland. I can't do that to you. You have a life here. You have friends and a family and I can't take that away from you. If you left—if you closed the gates to this world—everyone here would forget you ever existed. Could you do that to them? Could you close off the memories of another?"

I didn't know how to respond to that. That was definitely something I would have to think about, but I wasn't just going to say no. I had a lot to consider.

"But what about Alice having the powers to shape Wonderland? And all that?"

"That is why we can't leave you alone until then. Someone else might try to kidnap you and force you to make Wonderland into what they want."

"So I'm just a liability?"

"No, that's not what I meant."

"Then what did you mean?"

I reached out for me but I stepped back. "If you don't want me to stay in Wonderland, then why are you even bothering being my boyfriend?"

His eyes widened and then turned somber. "I don't know… I know I shouldn't have gotten this close to you, but I cared for you…"

"Then why won't you let me stay?"

"Because you could have regrets and would have to live with them for an eternity. I don't think you understand what it's like to live with regrets for the rest of your life when your life is as long as ours."

He had a point I knew, but it still wasn't his decision. I looked down. "I think… then I think maybe we should stop dating." As I said those words, I felt as if I were being stabbed in my heart. But if I were to leave, if he was going to force me out, it would be easier now than waiting later.

"I guess you are right. There is no point in dating if you will leave in the end. I'm sorry for not saying it sooner and for leading you on like I did. I guess me staying in Wonderland now is the best things." He smiled an ironic smile and kissed the top of my head. "I'll see you around, Alice."

With that, he headed towards his locker. Tears

started to drip down my face as I turned to head to my locker. I found Chase staring at me. I jumped.

"Were you listening in?" I asked.

He stretched his head. "Well... I saw you two walk off and I wanted to make sure everything was fine. I'm sorry, I didn't meant to..."

I shrugged. "It's fine. It's not like you wouldn't have found out anyway."

"Alice, are you okay?"

I shook my head. "Not really, no."

"Do you want to go get ice cream and skip dance? I'm sure Becca would understand."

I nodded. "Yeah, actually. That sounds good."

He wrapped his arms around me and let me cry on his shoulder. "Alice, you can choose whatever world you want. It's not up to him. You got that? Just think through all the possibilities and I will be behind you no matter what."

I nodded by my eyes were still full of tears. Why couldn't Malcolm have said the same thing? Except, deep down, I understand why Malcolm didn't want me to face eternity with regret. Was regret like that even worse when one didn't grow old?

Or maybe there was something else going on that I didn't realize.

THANK YOU FOR READING

Thank you so much for reading! Readers like you make it possible for authors like me to write stories! If you could spare a moment and leave a review on Amazon, Goodreads, BookBub, and wherever you like to buy books, that would mean the world to me! It really helps authors like me to succeed in the publishing world.

Acknowledgements

I want to thank everyone who made this novel possible. A thank you to Annie at Victory Editing for helping with this project and to Tamara for helping me with content edits. Thank you to Biserka Designs for the amazing covers they have done for my books. And lastly, thank you to my husband and parents who are always supporting me.

I also want to say thank you to Becca at Tippy Toe Dance studio for letting me use you and your studio in my book! And a thank you to Scott and Maria at Escape Fiction for letting me include you in my book as well! My high school years were amazing because of all three of you, and I am glad I got to include it in this series!

About the Author

Dani Hoots is a science fiction, fantasy, romance, and young adult author who loves anything with a story. She has a B.S. in Anthropology, a Masters of Urban and Environmental Planning, a Certificate in Novel Writing from Arizona State University, and a BS in Herbal Science from Bastyr University.

Currently she is working on a YA urban fantasy series called Daughter of Hades, a YA urban fantasy series called The Wonderland Chronicles, a historic fantasy vampire series called A World of Vampires, and a YA sci-fi series called Sanshlian Series. She has also started up an indie publishing company called FoxTales Press. She also works with Anthill Studios in creating comics through Antik Comics.

Her hobbies include reading, watching anime, cooking, studying different languages, wire walking, hula hoop, and working with plants. She is also an herbalist and sells her concoctions on FoxCraft Apothecary. She lives in Phoenix with her husband and visits Seattle often.

Feel free to email her with any questions you might
have!
danihootsauthor@gmail.com